Nature Trail Stories

Shannon McLeod

Nature Trail Stories
Copyright © 2023 Shannon McLeod
All rights reserved.

No part of this publication may be reproduced, distributed, or transmitted in any form or by any means, including photocopying, recording, or other electronic or mechanical methods, without the prior written permission of the publisher, except in brief quotations embodied in critical reviews, citations, and literary journals for noncommercial uses permitted by copyright law.

This is a work of fiction. Names, characters, businesses, places, events, locales, and incidents are either the products of the author's imagination or used in a fictitious manner. Any resemblance to actual persons, living or dead, or actual events is purely coincidental.

ISBN-13: 979-8-9861105-4-7
Cover art by Maxine Krispinsky
Cover design by Josh Dale
Author photo by Billy Hunt
Edited by Josh Dale & Kat Giordano
Printed in the U.S.A.

For more titles and inquiries, please visit:
www.thirtywestph.com

Trailheads

Waiting 7

Boys to Men 11

If I Said Everything I Thought 21

In Tandem 30

Pervert 34

Human Bridge 38

The Dog 46

Human Song 51

When a Woman Walks Alone 54

With Gun 57

After Leaving 59

Easier to Convince 64

Acknowledgments 93

About the Author 97

About the Publisher 99

Nature Trail Stories

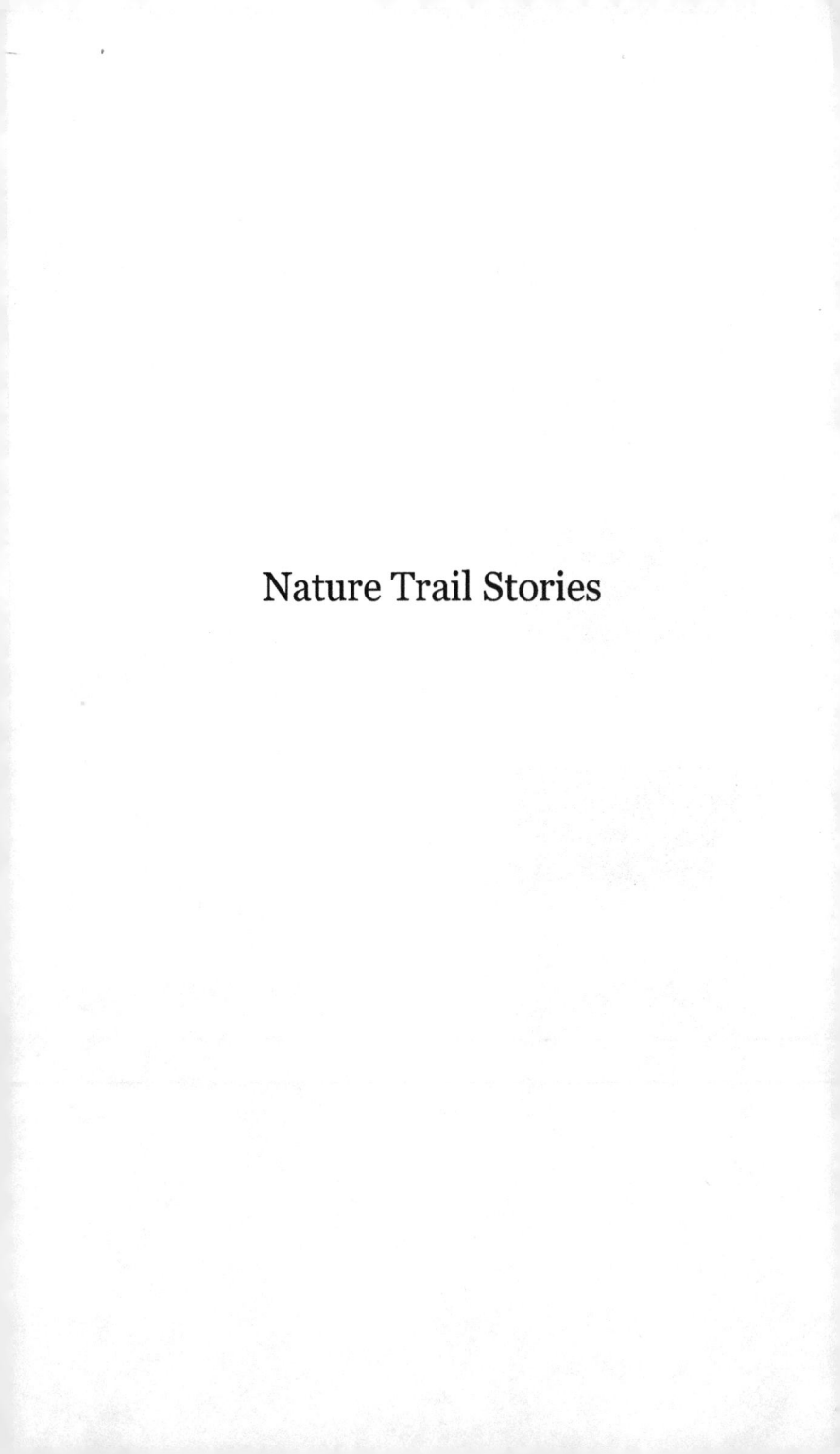

Waiting

I PULL IN beside the picnic shelter of the nearby nature center. There's a bench in front of the cage where the Northern Saw-whet Owl lives. It's usually where I sit after work when I'm feeling despondent. Today it's lower sixties, warm for March, but there's wind and cloud cover, so it might as well be fifty. I wrap my scarf around my neck a second time and approach the cage. My eyes revisit the story of the bird found along the highway, awake in the daytime, with a broken wing. They do not name their birds. The signs say names anthropomorphize the animals, which is supposedly a bad thing.

I find yellow eyes within his enclosure. He waddles from his bed of hay towards the perch. He is a small breed and appears infant-like despite being a full-grown adult. I think how if this were a story, the owl would begin to talk. He would give me some vague task, a challenge. He might say the name of a location over and over again. Maybe he'd hoot, "Louvre, Louvre, Loooouvre." Then I'd go home, pack my bags, and when my husband came upstairs to question the luggage, I'd throw him some trite phrase only Nic Cage would utter. I'd follow a series of clues: at every crossroads, an owl would appear, flying in the direction I was to follow.

In a cramped French boutique I'd find a vintage barrette shaped like an owl. I'd use it to sweep the hair from my eyes and no longer think of myself as Marcie, but rather The Owl Woman.

By the time I'd make it to the museum, I'd search it over the course of several days. You'd think there'd be more owls in such a large collection of art. Finally, I'd find a painting that would make me stop short and gasp, then push my face as close as it could get without tripping the alarm. It would be a dramatic oil on wood, depicting the same little, broken-winged talking bird from the nature preserve perched upon a familiar-looking washing machine—a washing machine in my own basement.

~

The owl opens his mouth as if to speak, and I jerk back a little. He picks under his wing with his beak. I sit down on the bench. I try a breathing technique that's supposed to bring contentment. I hear a thunk and feel a reverberation in the wood slab that travels through my slacks. A walnut, like a dense, vengeful softball, rolls off the bench and onto the ground. I pick it up and look at the walnut tree it came from. It's seemingly too far west to land so close to me. I think how if it'd fallen five inches closer it would have hit me on the scalp, maybe knocked me out.

If this were a story, a girl scout troop leader working in the community garden would walk by on her way to the outhouse and find me. I'd wake in an examination room surrounded by my loved ones. The doctor would enter and reveal X-rays, taken while I was still unconscious: tumors, shaped like cauliflower florets, only bigger.

Upon returning home, we would review the purpose of our savings. We'd take a trip to Disney World and my children would forget they were teenagers who were afraid to be seen with me long enough to enjoy a dozen rounds on Space Mountain. We'd spring for the souvenir magnet with a picture of us, screaming our heads off even though it was already round eleven.

My girls would look at the magnet longingly as they opened the fridge to get their own breakfast in the mornings I still had left. They would not forget to say they loved me before they went to school.

~

I'm getting cold, and I need to move. I get up and walk around the cages. I don't like the eagle, who seems like a bitch (though I know I'm anthropomorphizing like I shouldn't). I gaze lovingly at the turkey vultures: the red of their raw, ugly faces hiding rather gentle eyes. I notice tiny bones next to their water dish.

I walk towards the pine trees, along the trail. At first it's dotted with posts that uphold informational plaques about Michigan's native trees. Then the plaques disappear and the roots rise up from the narrowing path. If this were a story, a man would jump behind me and clasp a calloused hand over my mouth. In a flood of adrenaline I'd jab my elbow into his ribs. I'd summon combat moves I'd never really learned, only heard about on the network that calls itself "Television for Women." Even though I could never before imagine gouging out someone's eyes, I'd suddenly know what to do, and I'd pluck them clean from their sockets.

After calling the cops and giving a statement, foil blanket around my shoulders, I'd return home. They'd know not to ask about dinner by the look on my face. They'd never ask about dinner again, actually.

I'd feel an internal shift the next day. And I'd radiate a strength I always knew I had but could never externally convey. Coworkers at the dental office would notice, and patients, too. I'd no longer find Yelp reviews of Dr. Morris's practice that referred to me as "that meek woman at the front desk." I'd have confidence in my decisions, a sense of superiority.

~

The trail ends at a tree tagged with red spray paint. It is one marked for removal. I turn around, circle back around the bird cages. I return to my car. I turn on the ignition, but only to get the heat going. I'll wait here for a bit longer, I think. I'm waiting for something to happen to me, something to reveal myself.

Boys to Men

THE AIR WAS COLD and misty when Garrett completed his first lap around the pond. Yesterday he walked four laps around the 1.2 mile trail, and today his goal was six, in spite of the hangover.

~

Drew kept buying him beers last night, and Garrett hadn't refused. Drew rubbed his stubbly head as he updated his friend on the most recent signs that his marriage was trending downwards. Two months ago Drew's wife had cut off all her hair, and then she started building sleeves of tattoos, a new nonsense image on an arm each week. Drew said the latest was a portrait of Robert Stack, the host of *Unsolved Mysteries*.

"So much money," Drew said.

"For something so stupid." Garrett completed the thought for his friend.

Drew was avoiding home, avoiding the reality of a wife who was actively growing apart from him. Garrett thought being single was okay if this was the alternative. He was sad for Drew, but he also felt a small comfort at being the one who had it "together" in their friendship. Garrett asked if Drew had confronted Lina about these changes in behavior. Drew said no, he had a feeling she wouldn't tell him the truth anyway.

"Just try," Garrett said. "Worst case scenario: she'll

brush it off, maybe lie. But at least you can read her body language when she reacts to you."

Drew said he would do it, but at the end of the night, Garrett was pretty sure he wouldn't.

~

It was mostly women walking their dogs in the mornings on the trail, a whole slew of them today because it was Saturday. He said hello and smiled at them. The older women generally made eye contact and responded in kind. The younger ones sort of grimaced, a look of tension about their faces when they saw this six foot five, three hundred pound guy barreling towards them. Or they kept their eyes down, pretending not to hear him over whatever murder podcast was playing from their earbuds.

Maybe they really didn't hear him. He was trying to be less of the "Worst Case Scenario Guy," as Drew called him. Garrett brushed off the nickname initially, thinking it solely in reference to his tendency to overuse the phrase. But, since he'd started walking, he had more time to be with his thoughts. He realized that what he'd thought of as optimism actually ran in shades of negativity.

No more of that. He was going to keep up his end of the bargain. He would start exercising, lose some weight, and Mom would quit smoking to hold up her end. Garrett and his mom had begun texting each other daily check-ins. They were a small yet comforting addition to his day.

Do your laps?

Yeah, four. Buy your gum?

Yep, thirteen days without a smoke.

For once, there weren't other, more desperate, questions lurking beneath her inquiries.

When he walked on weekdays, before his evening

shifts at the nursing home, he usually stopped at the dock to sing. He'd listen to his voice skid off the algae-blooming water and feel a shiver of joy at the sound. Today, there was a man and his toddler son trying to fish. They pulled a minnow out of the water, and Garrett wondered if that was the bait or the catch.

Halfway through his fifth lap, Garrett noticed Slim Shady, which was what he called the heron that hung around the pond. He got out his phone to take a picture. As he lifted it, Slim pulled in his neck and lowered himself closer to the water, collapsing into a gray bulb. The photos he took of the bird came out fuzzy. He seemed close, but once Garrett zoomed adequately, the image was all ugly pixels. Against the shore, on a fallen sycamore, he saw a jacket. Then something brown and ratty. It was hair, with a whole person attached to it. A man was curled up, crouched by the water's edge, with his head resting on the bark of the felled tree beside the stump.

He must have been several yards away, but Garrett could smell the guy. He smelled like Wayne, old smoke and sour liquor emanating from his pores. Garret backed away, snapping a twig in the process. The man didn't flinch or react to the noise.

~

As a kid, Garrett was certain he'd be a famous singer. He was obsessed with Boys II Men; his room was surrounded in CD cover art unfolded and Scotch taped to his walls. It was from Boys II Men that he'd learned how to sing, how to harmonize. And then came the boy band craze: N*Sync, Backstreet Boys, 98 Degrees. He loved them all. By that time, though, he was in the sixth grade, and the other boys in class called these groups "gay." "So gay!" he agreed, laughing along. But secretly, known only to his mother who would drive him to Sam Goody, he'd spend his allowance on all the boy band CDs.

He noticed how girls most adored the highest pitched singers, the Nick Carters and the Justin Timberlakes. Garrett's voice changed early; he was one of the few baritones in the middle school choir. And while this led his music teacher, Ms. Heny, to dote on him, he wished he could be a tenor, an alto, even. He didn't want to be a Lance Bass.

While Garrett was practicing "It's So Hard to Say Goodbye to Yesterday" in his bedroom, Wayne was getting drunk behind the 7-Eleven. By junior year, Wayne had taken to stealing vodka from the liquor store and putting it in water bottles to bring to school. Garrett only realized this later. When it was happening, he chalked the ever-present odor up to his big brother's cologne. Wayne showered himself in Nautica Blue, which Garrett assumed was the reason for the sharp alcohol smell.

Garrett craved a closeness with Wayne that Wayne couldn't offer. He'd eavesdrop on his sister and her friends from their phone extension in the basement, awed by their vulnerability with each other. They shared their greatest insecurities and then assured the other how cute and smart they were. He thought that Wayne should be this to him, and he resented that he wasn't.

Then, after Wayne's third suspension and his sessions with Dr. Charles, who Garrett later learned was a psychologist, Wayne suddenly became interested in his little brother's life. Garrett was thrilled when Wayne said, "Sure," he would come to his brother's choir concert.

Ms. Heny wouldn't allow him to peek into the audience from backstage. She said it might psych him out.

He listened to her. She seemed to be the only teacher worth listening to. It was December, and Ms. Heny disregarded the tradition of public school winter concerts' including holiday songs from a variety of cultures and instead filled the program exclusively with Christmas songs. He had a solo in "O Holy Night."

As the students filed up to the risers, he looked out on the audience. He couldn't quite make out the faces with the house lights down, the stage lights up. They sang "Let it Snow," and Garrett's face turned red when he swayed the wrong way for the choreography. He was so distracted by the thought of Wayne there, watching him. He hoped his blushing wasn't visible from the audience.

Then, halfway through the song from *Home Alone*, the song he most enjoyed singing, he heard the door open, and a rectangle of light poured in from the hallway. He could hear the crinkling of winter coats as people turned around in their seats. The students were all looking at the interloper, which led even Ms. Heny to glance back as she conducted.

"Sorry, sorry!" Wayne's voice cut through the music.

Once the song was over, the applause felt like a sigh of relief. An audio reset button.

Next, his solo. Garrett stepped down from the risers and met the microphone just steps from Ms. Heny.

"Yeeeah! That's my baby brother!" Wayne's voice ripped through the auditorium. Garrett began to sing, and Wayne stopped. Then "Gary!" Garrett's nickname which was bequeathed to him after his first wedgie and would accompany future wedgies and noogies and every time Wayne would grab Garrett's forearms and force Garrett to slap himself.

Wayne started chanting, "Ga-ry Ga-ry Ga-ry" like a

Jerry Springer Show taunt. He turned around when he noticed no one was joining him. "What's wrong with you?" Wayne asked no one in particular or everyone around him. Garrett saw vague movement in the audience, and he could only assume it was Wayne, getting up for god knows what reason. Soon, Wayne was in the aisles. He pulled a lighter from his pocket and held the flame up, as though at a rock concert. Garret continued singing, but his voice cracked. He was half a beat behind. He saw Mr. Sheffield rise from the first row to escort his brother out.

~

Garrett returned to the path and continued on. He'd be back soon, anyway, he thought. There was no rush. The man wasn't going anywhere. He'd walk another lap while he decided what to do. The clouds were low and gray, pressing down on his brain. It occurred to him that it might not be all hangover, this feeling. When the sky was filled with low clouds, he often had the sensation that a too-heavy wool blanket was draped over his gray matter. He tried not to let the weather affect his mood, but it did. As a child on rainy days, his father would scold him for his sullen mood. "Go play with your brother. Wayne doesn't let the rain spoil his fun."

He came upon a short couple, wearing jackets in nearly the same shade of teal. Garrett wondered if they recognized they were matching or if they were the kind of couple who'd grown so similar that they could no longer notice their sameness. The couple walked slowly. Garrett slowed himself down, staying a dozen paces behind. He hoped that the couple would notice the man and, in their superior twoness of logic, would know what to do. Perhaps they'd take care of the situation and Garrett could go on walking, get his six laps in and move on with his day.

Slim Shady stretched his neck up again, swiveled his head as he flicked his wings out, then pulled them back in, adjusting his position. His eyes were black and watchful. The woman pointed to the bird, and the man said "Yeah." They were observant, at least.

Garrett's pocket vibrated. Mom: *I'm watching Mad Men and now I really want a smoke.*

Don't watch Mad Men, he replied. As though it were all so easy. As though he hadn't nearly ordered a Denny's omelet from Grub Hub instead of getting up to walk his laps this morning.

He added, *TV is the worst. I can't watch commercials anymore. Too many glistening hot wings and levitating burger patties.* Used to be they mostly talked about Wayne. Was he in rehab again? Was he using? Did he get a new job? Was he still living with those deadbeat friends?

~

College was a chance for Garrett to disengage from the drama of his family and find drama of his own choosing. He auditioned for the acapella group after he'd seen them perform on the quad during orientation. He was intimidated. He'd been passed over for all the male leads in his high school musicals, and he'd lost confidence in his singing abilities. But he thought, *Worst case scenario: I won't make the cut.* At least he'd know whether to keep pursuing or give up on music for good. He made it in.

Garrett fell in love with singing again, and also with a woman. Alison always wore pastel colors. At first Garrett found this adorable. He'd watch her during rehearsals from the opposite side of their semicircle, and her colors would set her apart, a daisy among the sea of navy blue university hoodies. Once they broke up and she started dating Ian, her wardrobe choices became obnoxious to Garrett. The annoyance was made even greater on the days when she wore her hair in pigtails. *Grow up already*, he thought.

During an overnight trip for an out-of-state competition, he was stuck in the same hotel room as Ian. He woke to Alison sneaking in. He listened to whispering from across the room but couldn't decipher the words. Garrett switched on his bedside lamp and gathered his things into his duffel bag. On his way out, he saw that Alison had pulled the covers over her head—hiding or pretending to hide. He drove home alone that night. That was the end of singing groups for him.

~

The couple passed the leaning boxelder, where Garrett sometimes saw turtles sunning themselves. The tree limb was bare today, and it marked the spot just before the man. Garrett kept looking between the couple and the shoreline, waiting for them to notice the man, waiting for their reaction. He saw the unnatural beige lump of cloth. He saw the couple reach around each other's waists and veer closer to the outside edge of the trail.

Garrett's tongue filled with the rusty taste that flushed his mouth when he got angry. *Those people, unwilling to interrupt their nice little walk to help a man in need.* Garrett stopped. He checked his phone out of habit, as he did in any moment of stillness. His fingers combed the curly strands of his beard. A gray whippet wearing little dog booties and a sweater trotted by, followed by a terribly thin woman. He scowled at them as they, too, passed without regard for the man huddled by the mucky shore.

Worst case scenario, he thought, *the guy won't want any help and I'll just go on with my laps.* Then, at least, he wouldn't have to feel guilty. He wouldn't have to think, *What if.*

Garrett approached the man with less caution this time. "Hey, man," he announced his presence. The man didn't turn, but he grunted a "Hey." As Garrett came nearer, he saw that the man's foot had sunk into the muck. His muddied tennis shoe must have been totally waterlogged. But the man hadn't moved. In fact, as Garrett inspected it closer, he noticed the man's bare ankle. Sitting atop it, a slick black leech. Garrett didn't have any salt, but he thought if it had just crawled up, it might not have latched yet. He pinched the slimy digit and pulled. The leech came off, and blood rushed out with it.

"Ay!" the man's voice sounded clearer now, and he pulled his foot from the water. Garrett flicked the leech back into the pond.

"Sorry. It was a leech." Garrett looked at the man, whose eyes were open now, bloodshot, looking like Wayne's, he thought. Wayne's eyes were brown, though, and this man's were green. When you had someone on your mind and you didn't want them inside your brain, they had a way of taking shape in the physical world around you. "Let me help you," Garrett said. He didn't want the man to think he was just here to inflict pain. Garrett held out his forearm. The man looked up at him but didn't move. "Let's get you up, buddy. There's a shelter just a ways up the road." Garrett grabbed the man's upper arm and tried to hoist him to his feet.

"Fucker!" the guy mumbled. Garrett was pretty sure it's what the guy said. "Where do you think I came from?" the man said more clearly.

"Fine, asshole." Garrett pushed his elbow away, and the man caught his fall in the sandy soil. He resumed the hunched position Garrett had found him in initially.

Garrett thought of his last conversation with Wayne. How he proposed all the ideas he had for his brother's life: the places he could stay, the jobs he could pursue, the family members he could reconnect with. Wayne argued the drawbacks of each of these proposed plans, and Garrett left the conversation feeling rejected, almost scolded.

The man closed his eyes. At least his foot was now clear out of the scummy pond water.

Garrett walked away, towards a bench beside the dock. He wanted to see the small movements around him while he sat still for a moment. The father and son were there, but now they were packing up their gear. The little boy looked forlorn. Hovering over the water, their voices carried, and Garrett heard the man tell his son that the fish must be sleeping in today.

Garrett got out his phone and texted Drew, *How's it going.*

Good, man. I think things are back to normal with Lina.

That's great. Did you talk with her, then?

Nah, but today it just feels like she loves me again, you know? I think it was a phase.

Garrett thought for a moment as he watched the mosquitos land on the pond, creating tiny dimples that appeared and disappeared.

Glad to hear it, he wrote.

He walked on. He had almost reached his goal. His abdomen filled with minnows.

If I Said Everything I Thought

I MADE PANCAKES while listening to my station, which played nothing but Grateful Dead each Saturday morning. After every other song one DJ would say to another, "What do you think of that big old hunk of tunage?"

I liked hearing them talk. Before the pandemic, before lockdown, these interludes were annoying. "Just bring back the tunage already!" I'd say, flicking the spatula like a whip. And Marshall would chime in, "They're not gonna answer you, Mom. It's a radio."

"I don't need someone to answer for me to talk. I talk to you, don't I?" That was one of my usual replies and Marshall would usually smirk.

The DJs were a good reminder of how conversations go. Ones that weren't purely life updates, but those discussions of shared experiences. The kind I never knew were comforting before their absence.

I listened to podcasts for the same reason. I didn't really care what they were talking about, as long as the hosts were playful with each other in a way that sounded genuine and kind.

I talked to Marshall, but he was always staring at his phone or computer. When I repeated myself while waving my hand between his face and the screen, he'd get all pissy and snap back a minimal reply.

I talked to my cats, Caesar and Brutus. They didn't get along. Caesar mostly lived under the couch.

The workers had the weekend off, so I was getting a break from the incessant hammering as they replaced the siding on our house. One of them was stout. He wore camo pants and whistled a lot. The other one was taller and never smiled, just smoked and flicked his cigarette butts all over my lawn. They argued sometimes, but I didn't know about what because I didn't speak Spanish. I'd forgotten nearly all four years of classes in high school.

Early last week, the smoker stalked away from the whistler after one of their heated exchanges. He lit a cigarette in front of my kitchen window. He looked off into the sycamores that separated our yard from the neighbor's. I thought he might need cheering up, so I picked up Brutus from his food bowl and held him by the window. I knocked on the glass until the smoker turned around. I grabbed Brutus's paw and moved it like he was waving. The smoker shook his head dismissively, but he smiled, too.

For the next few days, I'd glance out my office window to watch them. When the hammering ceased, I'd take a break from work and go down to the kitchen. I'd grab Brutus and say hello as the smoker smoked. The smoker would wave and smile, then turn away. My heart pounded like I'd just hit on a stranger in public. I'd smile for the next half hour or until I encountered Marshall and he'd ask what was so funny.

~

I made Marshall sit at the table with me if he wanted to eat my food. I'd given up on fighting for him to leave his phone in his room during mealtimes, though. I looked at him for a while, expression changing in reaction to whatever it was he scrolled through.

"What?" He said when he caught me staring.

I took a bite of pancakes. "Nothing," I said with a full mouth.

"You're so creepy," he said. I petted his hair and looked out the window. I missed the smoker.

~

Later that evening, I was on the phone with my mother. I wasn't really listening. Instead, I was focusing on my pelvic floor exercises. My physical therapist told me to imagine I was picking up a blueberry with my vagina. She was probably somewhere between twenty-five and twenty-nine. No ring on her finger. I wanted to mention something about how a ten-pound baby had passed through there and maybe I ought to imagine a more realistic-sized fruit. But she struck me as sensitive, like me. I didn't want to imply that she was bad at her job. I didn't say anything about the blueberry. But as I was listening to my mother, I imagined picking up an apricot with my vagina.

"Oh, that's awful. I'm sorry," I said, assuming she was describing an ailment.

"What? Are you listening to me?"

"Sorry."

"What are you doing?" She could usually guess by the background noise.

"My PT exercises."

"What for?"

"It hurts when I sit, Mom."

"That's because it's all you do."

I could remind her that I was working from home, so of course I sat in front of the computer all day, but it wasn't worth it. What would life be like for me if I said everything I thought, like she did?

"How's Marshall?" She changed the subject.

"I don't know, I never see him."

"How can that be? He lives in your house, Eileen."

"The only time he ever leaves his room is to take walks."

"Go with him. Perfect opportunity for you to get some exercise."

"He's a teenager; he doesn't want to take walks with me. He doesn't want to be *seen* with me."

My phone chimed and a notification box popped up, signaling an incoming video call from See for Me, the app where people with visual impairments called to get help from seeing users. I felt the thrill of being needed. I told my mom I had to go help a blind person. She laughed like I was joking, and I hung up.

The video feed came in. A glass coffee table with two sets of feet underneath. The coffee table had a series of liquids on it: a diet coke, a liquor bottle wrapped in a paper bag, a bottle of Pepto Bismol. I assumed I would be asked to read the contents of one of these bottles. As a man greeted me hello, I wondered why the second pair of feet wasn't doing the seeing for him.

"Hello, my name is Greg," he said.

I said my name was Eileen and asked what I could help him with.

"Could you count some money for me, please?" He held a wad of cash awkwardly in one hand, the phone aiming in front of him with the other. He unrolled a series of twenty-dollar bills onto the coffee table. I recited the quantities, "Another twenty." He'd repeat and I'd confirm. He mumbled something about thinking he had some tens, too. He apologized for taking so long to unfurl his money.

The other man, with exposed toes in a pair of slides under the glass shifted his feet and chuckled. I said something about how we needed different sized bills in this country, like in every other country. He apologized again, and I regretted the comment. I had meant it as a complaint on behalf of the visually impaired rather than the ones helping the visually impaired, as myself. Then he showed a series of tens, and I told him what each bill was worth. He said that was it and thanked me again, told me to stay healthy.

He must have thought I'd hung up already because they started talking about pills. It occurred to me why he needed third party confirmation of this money. I hung up, feeling a mixture of shame and guilt. Like I'd been caught snooping around in my son's room.

The drier buzzed and I went downstairs to restart it. The ancient thing needed three cycles to get anything dry. Marshall had just come in from a walk. His head was in the fridge.

"You hungry?"

He flinched, then closed the fridge slowly. "Hmm?" He turned around, sloth-like. The sun had gone down since I'd last been downstairs. I turned on the kitchen light and he flinched again. His eyes looked red. I gave him a questioning look.

"What?" he laughed and put his face into the refrigerator again. I leaned over him to grab a box of cereal from the top of the fridge. His hair smelled like my college dorm.

I stood beside him, waiting for him to say something, waiting to decide if I'd say something.

"What?" he said again, defensive this time.

"Your hair. It's getting so long." I tried to smile.

"Well, I'm not letting you cut it." He closed the fridge and kept his gaze on the floor.

"No, I like it. Your father used to wear his hair longer like that when we were in college."

He smiled a bit, darted a glance up. "I know."

~

I called my mom back because I didn't know what else to do. I was going to tell her about what I'd just witnessed—or helped facilitate—on See for Me, but explaining the app would take too long and I'd lose my patience. I told her that Marshall just came home smelling like weed. "What should I do, Mom?" I was horrified.

Mom laughed. "You do what I did. You pretend you don't smell anything. You leave him be. You let him grow up and figure things out for himself."

~

I told my neighbor about the video call transaction as we were both gardening the next day. "What are people doing buying drugs during a pandemic?" I said.

"What are people doing not buying drugs during a pandemic?" she answered.

"It made me worried about Marshall. These guys were young. How do I know he's not off buying and taking drugs on his walks?" I didn't disclose to Joyce that I had, in fact, smelled pot on him. Just that Marshall was keeping himself shut up in his room and then slipping outside for nightly walks around the neighborhood.

"Is he like that with his father? All secretive and stuff?"

"I don't know. His father would like me to believe they have the perfect relationship. So, I'll never get the real story." I appreciated that Joyce knew not to say Dave's name. Even though Dave was still close with her husband.

"My mom thinks I should feign ignorance. But I think I should just ask him about it. Isn't it better to open a dialogue?" I pulled up grass because I'd run out of weeds to pick.

"Our parents are a different generation. We're closer with our kids. It's better, I think. They're more comfortable being honest with us."

~

That night, I sorted through old mail cluttered on the counter. Three credit cards thunked to the bottom of the trash with the weight of unearned responsibility. Marshall came flopping down the stairs, cargo pockets jangling. I loved or reviled his loud thunking steps depending upon my mood.

"Hey, I thought I'd order pizza tonight," I said.

He retrieved his jacket from the closet. "Nice. I'll take jalapeños on my half. Can we get the thick crust?"

"Sure," I said because I was too focused on my next statement to recognize that he'd gotten his way on the crust he liked and I hated. "Wait, honey. I have a question for you."

Marshall turned around. He wiggled his nose the way he did when he had dried snot in there.

"What you do on your walks—can I join you sometime?" I looked up from a Bed Bath & Beyond catalog.

"What do you mean?" he said quietly.

I tossed the catalog and threw my head to one side. I held my pointer and thumb together in front of my mouth and sucked the invisible joint. "You know, some mother-son bonding?" I tried to laugh it off.

He itched his nostril and shook his head. "Do you know how inappropriate that is?" He sounded like he was mimicking his teacher.

"Sorry!" I held my hands up in surrender like I did so often with him now.

He turned around and stood in silence a while. Then he made a full turn back to me. "You can walk with me." He let out a sigh. "But I am not smoking with you."

I let him lead the way and we looped the neighborhood. Then we cut between two houses' lawns on a narrow dirt path. There was a retention pond at the end of it. I pointed out a turtle on a log, enjoying the waning evening sun.

"That's Michelangelo," he said. A childish glee overtook his face.

I could feel my eyes well. I wanted to pull him close to me, squeeze his skinny body into my expanding one. But I also wanted to be allowed to walk with him again.

We went back the way we came, and I resisted the urge to grab his hand. He told me about his online classes. I tried to listen intently without asking too many questions.

Life was cruel. Your child gave you this whole new experience of love. On a higher plane, one you didn't even know existed before. And then you had to hold it back, pretend you didn't feel it coursing in you all rabid and wild when you looked at them sometimes. That he didn't seem to want it anymore—that my love scared him or repulsed him—was too painful.

~

With the siding finished the next day, the workers were packing up. They hauled away the ladders, one of them on each end. I rushed to the window with Brutus.

"You're a psycho, Mom." Marshall came in and said.

The smoker glanced up, but both of his arms were occupied so he couldn't wave. "You never know. Maybe this is his favorite part of the day," I said, waving Brutus's paw. I think I saw the smoker smile, but his eyes were already downcast again.

"That guy's day or the cat's day?"

"That guy."

"He probably has a life." My son peeled a clementine over the sink.

I told Marshall he was probably right. I let Brutus go and he ran away quickly, the way he does when I hold him too long.

In Tandem

PERSON RIDES their bicycle to therapy. It's a tandem. They have added outdated science textbooks to the basket in back to weigh down the empty half of the bike. Person picked the books up from the school's dumpster last week. The school marks the halfway point to work, and now it also marks where they picked up old books, and the time when the books became necessary.

Therapist is too chipper. A self-proclaimed athlete, her biceps stretch the armholes of her polyester polo. She probably plays tennis on days when she wants to "take it easy." Person is talking about their coworkers: the one who is passive-aggressive and the other who is just aggressive. Therapist urges Person to be gentle with themself. Person brings up their mother because they don't know what else to say. Suddenly, the sound of screaming. Stomping. A string of expletives like an incantation.

"Sorry about that," Therapist chuckles without a trace of discomfort on her face. "That's group therapy in the room next door."

Person cannot bring themself to talk about the breakup with Therapist, who has clearly never been rejected. Person has this realization after they hear a guttural scream from the other side of the office wall, beyond the hyacinth which somehow never wilts.

After this session, Person hangs around the parking

lot. First, they pretend to fiddle around with the bike lock, eyes darting up to the office door at grandfather clock intervals. Eventually, they take a seat at the picnic table. They inspect the worn wood because they've left their phone at home. The sense of timelessness is disorienting but comfortable. The word *PERFECTIONISM* is carved in all capital letters and then crossed out with a gouge. *I free myself from my story of myself* is written in permanent marker against the grain.

Then, the sound of the door opening. Five people scatter in different directions without goodbyes, as though they're all exiting a grocery store. Guy walks in Person's direction. They perk up, say hello. Guy looks around. He sweeps his head, like he's just making sure the hello wasn't for him. He turns back to Person. "Oh, hi." He halts his swift pace.

Person asks if he likes group therapy. "I'm thinking of trying it," they add to minimize his potential defensiveness. "Individual therapy just isn't for me," they say to show they are equally vulnerable to the world.

He comes closer. "It's good. Really good."

"I've heard screaming."

He steps a leg over the bench and takes a seat at the picnic table across from Person. "It's not about the screaming, it's about other people being there to witness your screams."

Person nods. This picnic table seems to be an extension of the therapists' office.

"It opens you up to peace and kindness, knowing your anger is accepted."

Person asks if they can join. Guy says it's too late; the group started last month and won't open up for a new cohort until next fall. He says he will witness Person's screams, though. He says the best place to scream is on the river.

Person takes the textbooks out of the basket, stacks them on the table.

"Are you worried about those?" he asks. "You can leave them in my car if you want." Person says no. They try to get the tandem into his car, but it won't fit.

Person sits on the front seat of their bike and welcomes Guy on the back seat. His weight is greater than the textbooks. He makes it so Person must push harder on the pedals. But the bike is steadier, too, not jostling over potholes. Guy shouts directions as they enter traffic. They turn onto a residential street. Person sees his pointing hand in their peripheral vision. There's a narrow dirt path, parting the tree line. The bike bumps over roots and rocks. Branches whip their elbows. Guy tells Person to slow down, and they come to the river. Dust kicks up as they brake. They get off the bike and Person props up the kickstand. They walk to the water.

"Is there a special way to do this?"

"Yes, but you'll know when you're ready."

Person gulps air and then screams. The water ripples where fish are traveling or maybe just the soundwaves of their screaming. When Person is empty enough for now, they turn to Guy. Guy nods.

They both sit down, setting their feet in the sandy dirt at the water's edge. There's foamy buildup at the shore that reminds Person of root beer floats, which they loved so much in childhood and haven't tasted since. The water is a rich brown, its color deepened by dead leaves and animal feces. Person takes a deep breath, and the sweet, rotten smell almost makes them sick. Beautiful things are sometimes repulsive and vice versa. Mosquitos are getting fat from Person's blood and they don't care. They no more feel the insect mouths than they would feel a single bristle scrub their back molar when brushing their teeth.

Guy and Person are silent for a while. Their hands planted in patchy grass. Guy yelps, a sputter of a scream, and Person hears it echo. Guy rubs his hands on his denim knees. Person thinks he is ready to push himself up. Instead, he holds his palm to Person, turns and gives them a look like, *Why not?* And—as though it's easy—Person takes his hand. They watch the geese bob through the gentle rapids and out of sight. The two hold a tiny bubble of warm space between their palms.

Pervert

I WAS WALKING around my housing complex, at the top of the hill, shaking a bag of cat treats. A little head popped through a bush at the bottom. I thought the movement was Frosting, my cat. But it was only a child, and she was walking up the hill towards me.

"Can I have some of those?" She pointed at the treat bag.

"These are for cats, not people."

"I know," she said. She wiped hair out her face, using her entire hand, all of her palm and all five fingers, the way little girls do. "I'm looking for a cat."

"Me too," I said, "What's your cat look like?"

"She's black."

"Mine's orange. His name is Frosting."

The child laughed in a way I found condescending.

"What's your cat's name?" I said, challenging her to do better.

"Nightmare Moon." She gave a single shrug that reminded me of bread popping up from a toaster. "It's from a show."

"Hm. I came up with Frosting myself." I looked around the courtyard we were in and shook the treats.

The little girl called, "Frosting! Nightmare Moon!" She alternated the names over and over. She wasn't prioritizing her lost cat over mine.

"I like Nightmare Moon," I conceded and emptied

treats into the girl's palm.

She was missing her two front teeth. I recalled my first-grade school picture, my tongue sticking out between my smile. I had no sense of children's ages. I should change my voice to a higher register with her, I thought, the way I talked to Frosting. I'd been speaking with this child like a peer.

There was a lady watching us from the bottom of the hill. She had dyed black hair with a thick strip of white at her scalp. The girl turned and waved. "That's my grandma," she said.

I suddenly worried that I shouldn't be talking to a little girl I didn't know. That this woman would think I was a pervert. But the lady walked into the house. She was not worried because I was a woman, and most women aren't perverts. Or they're not the kind of perverts who inflict harm on others. Women are the kind of perverts who inflict harm on themselves. And most guardians, it seemed, didn't worry about exposing their children to self-hatred.

The girl showed me her scraped knee, which was caked with dirt. A dried blade of grass dangled from the wound. If I were her grandmother, I would have made her wash that knee. I would have given her a peroxide-soaked cotton ball to sizzle it clean.

The girl followed me to Bitternut Road. It connected all the cul-de-sacs like an artery. I stepped on a walnut and slipped a little. "Ah, shit," I said, grabbing my lower back.

"Are you okay?" She walked around to face me and looked up with squinty eyes.

"I'm fine." I kept walking, hunched and holding my back. "I pulled a muscle trying to move my couch."

"I can help you move stuff. I'm strong." She grinned,

toothlessly.

I scowled at her. Then my mother's voice was coming out of my mouth, "Look at those little chicken wings! You can't be *that* strong."

We were at the farthest reaches of the complex: the courtyard where a line of trees separated homes from the interstate. The constant stream of cars sounded like the ocean. She crouched down and squealed as a black cat ran to her. She stood and the cat's bottom half hung from her folded arms. It looked uncomfortable, but the cat didn't seem to mind.

"Wow, she ran right to you," I said.

"That's 'cause she loves me!"

I scanned the perimeter of the courtyard. Still no Frosting. I called his name a few more times. My eyes got wet. I faced the wind to dry them.

"Doesn't Frosting miss you, you think?" she said, still holding her cat.

"Goddammit, cats don't miss humans. That cat didn't miss you!" The tears came streaming.

The girl, holding her cat, ran away. I wiped my face with my jacket. I walked the remaining half of the loop, shaking the bag of treats and calling my cat's name.

At home, I put a dish of wet food on the front porch. I lay down on the couch with my head by the window to keep watch. Eventually, I fell asleep.

When I woke up, I looked out the window into the morning. No Frosting. I opened the door to get a closer look, to see if any food was missing. When I did, a streak of orange fur scurried past me and into the house. I chased after and picked him up from his spot by the heating vent. His paw pads were cold against my skin. We returned to the couch, where I set him on my lap. I picked leaves from his long hair and he purred.

~

On my way home from the pet store after work, I drove past the bush where the little girl first appeared. I noticed a pink jump rope on a porch nearby, where her grandmother had stood. When I got inside, I put on Frosting's new harness.

I walked through the grass to the neighboring courtyard. I stepped past the jump rope, Frosting tight within my grasp, and knocked on the door. I saw the curtain waver. The door opened with a couple yanks, and the little girl peeked around the knob.

"I found Frosting. I thought you'd like to meet him."

"Nana says I can't play with you anymore." She closed the door.

Back home, I gave Frosting his dinner. I made myself a rum and root beer. When Frosting was finished eating, I took him onto the balcony in his harness, so we could safely enjoy the outdoors. I tied Frosting's leash to the railing, and he rubbed against it. Then he spotted something. His tail puffed up and his back arched. A black cat scurried through the trees.

"It's okay," I stroked him. "She's not gonna hurt you."

Human Bridge

"Walk on me," said the man lying on the gallery floor. "Let's try this out." He insisted he was part of this collection, and the "Human Bridge" was its centerpiece.

Molly's boss hadn't mentioned anything about a human bridge, but there had been a lot he didn't tell her, she was discovering throughout her first day on the job. Like what to say when the phone rang, for example. Or what to do if a homeless man took residence in the entryway, then came inside and left with the only roll of toilet paper.

She'd been so thrilled when she got the call with the job offer. It seemed ideal. She could work alone (she was thoroughly tired of people) and spend all day soaking up art. She hadn't paid attention to the fact that the gallery was almost exclusively landscapes. She hated landscapes. This town was obsessed with the surrounding mountains and overpriced mountain-climbing clothing. Molly couldn't comprehend why one would need reinforced hiking boots to go to the movies. At least the man lying on the ground, asking her to walk on him was interesting—if it was, indeed, art. The paintings encircling him were scenes from an autumn nature trail, the same orange-hued watercolors she'd seen a hundred times before. For the first instance of the day, Molly prayed for a phone call. She needed an excuse to step away, or at least an opportunity to look for documentation of said installation.

No such phone call occurred. From this angle, she could see crusted snot clinging to his nose hairs. He wasn't unattractive. But he had a worn out look to him that indicated he was different. She snapped the hair tie on her wrist that lay beside her watch. It was a habit. The snap soothed her. Molly stalled by asking what the human bridge signified.

"It represents our willingness to trod upon and destroy life when prompted by arbitrary human zoning, like nature trails and bridges."

It sounded like a legitimate artist statement: wordy bullshit. She was an expert on artist statements with a forty-thousand-dollar degree to prove it.

~

Fresh out of art school, Molly was still in the college town, like a loser who refuses to leave after the party is over. Her thesis collection was geometric and minimal. Louise was proud of her, she'd said. Louise was a brilliant sculptor. Molly worried it was obvious how much the shapes and patterns in Louise's own work had influenced Molly's paintings. Before she'd gotten to art school, she mainly painted flowers from photos she found online, sometimes dopey imitations of manga.

Molly was convinced she and Louise had a long stretch of eternity together. Which was in large part because Louise was her first real girlfriend.

Louise was a year younger, so she had one more year before graduation. Most people assumed Louise was older than Molly. Something about her tone of voice when she spoke.

In moments when Louise's condescension wore on her, Molly thought about how Louise had a stupid haircut.

It was a childish bob, which photos at her parents' house revealed had been her look since the sixth grade, at least. Sometimes Louise even put an infantile barrette in it, just above her right ear. Yet still, she realized, Molly was intimidated by her. Some people, no matter their physical stature, carry a power about them.

Molly's first dinner with Louise's parents was awkward. Her father was pleasant, but terse. Her mother had a way of talking that sounded harried, as though she were annoyed at everyone's presence. All her phrases were short, made shorter by speeding up at the end. "You want ice cream? You've gottahaveitalamode!"

Afterwards, when Louise reported that her mom "adored" her, Molly thought about it. This was just the way her mother was. Which brought Molly a feeling of closeness to Louise, to understand that this must be why *she* was the way she was. Louise cared for her in the way she knew how, Molly thought.

She remembered lying in her bed after the first time they had sex. Louise giggled. And after Molly questioned her several times about the cause of her laughter, Louise admitted it was due to Molly's clumsiness. She pried for a more detailed explanation. Louise described her sexual mishaps. Molly rolled onto her side and pretended to fall asleep.

The next few days, Molly spent every minute alone studying porn to educate herself. But it all felt so fake, the pleasure merely a performance.

~

The Human Bridge closed his eyes and relaxed into the floor. How some people could be so at ease in a public place was beyond her. "I need to use the restroom," Molly said and walked a bit too quickly to the unisex restroom. She washed her hands as she looked in the mirror, cheeks visibly flushed. Molly smiled. She'd always loved her teeth, which were naturally straight. She relished when people asked about having braces and she got to tell them she was lucky enough to not need them. Molly shook her hands dry, then clapped her palms against her cheeks. Her wristwatch caught in her hair, and she tried unwinding a strand from around the dial. She flinched when she plucked it from her scalp instead.

It was a gift from Louise, the only gift she'd picked out without Molly's input. (Molly disliked how Louise always *asked* what she wanted for her birthday and Christmas.) Louise had returned from the Salvation Army and offered her the watch, saying, "It looked like you." Molly found it so touching, to be on her mind enough that Louise had associated an object with her even when out of her presence. The watch was broken, Molly discovered after a new battery didn't get it ticking, but Molly still wore it daily. "It's like a bracelet," Molly said after Louise suggested tossing it.

~

When she left the bathroom, the man was still there, staring at the ceiling. The phone rang, and she ran to the office, heels clopping loudly.

"Hello?" she said, simply, out of habit.

"How's it going, Molly?" It was Glen, the gallery owner.

She shuffled around papers on the desk, looking for evidence of "The Human Bridge." She couldn't ask, couldn't reveal her ignorance or possible huge misstep. "Uh, good. Going well."

"Many patrons? Any sales?"

"Yeah, a few patrons. No sales yet."

Silence on his end of the line. *Was this abnormal? How many sales were typical?* Another bit of information Glen had failed to provide.

"But a couple came in, and they were really interested in one of the Van Broder pieces. They took a card and said they'd think about it."

"Hmm. Okay then."

Her heart hammered. The space heater under the desk blazed against her toes.

"Any questions?"

Molly looked around the room for some stack of toiletries. The office was a cluttered mess. "Um, I don't think so. Thanks." He hung up and her panic increased. Now she had to fix this all herself.

When she returned to the showroom, the man was still draped there. She watched him from a distance. His Carhartt jacket rose and fell with his breath. She could see his profile as he gazed at the ceiling. His cheeks were striped with mutton chops.

"Okay, show me how this works," she said, approaching. Molly decided to look at his face to determine whether to walk on him or not. If she detected any hint of gratification on his face, she wouldn't set foot on him. If she detected none, then she'd do it. For his sake. For both of their sakes.

He said to simply walk across his body, any way she liked. He said he was the object, and she was the change agent.

Molly stood by his feet. She asked him his name.

"I have no name." He said to the ceiling tiles.

She decided to believe this was further proof of his

legitimacy as an artist. She put one foot on him at the top of his thigh. She began to transfer her weight onto it, but her foot slipped. Her heel slid into the canyon of his groin. He made a low squeal and his face went pallid, but he kept his gaze fixed above him and said nothing.

She shifted her weight back to the foot on the floor.

"Go on," the man said.

Molly put both feet onto the floor. "I need to run an errand. Can you watch the place for five minutes?"

~

There was a pharmacy around the block. She would buy a few rolls of toilet paper, some paper towels, and then she'd be out of there. In-and-out before anyone else entered the gallery. The setting sun sent its rays into her eyes. She held her purse close to her body, a habit she didn't notice she had when walking in the city. The CVS was comforting to her at this moment: familiar and authoritative. This chain was here when you needed something essential in times of conflict. This store would save her.

And then, at the self-checkout: Crystal. Molly turned in the opposite direction and pretended to study the Coinstar machine. Then she sidestepped into the cosmetics, praying Crystal wouldn't notice her. Molly hadn't seen her since that night, and she had hoped she never would again. Molly could stuff down the guilt when there weren't reminders of Crystal's existence. But then, when there were—like, for instance, when they stood in the same pharmacy—she felt flooded with regret.

They only kissed. They both stayed too late at the party. They were drunk and Molly was trying to comfort Crystal, whose cousin had just killed himself. Had Molly told Louise, it would have been the end of them, she was sure. She felt as if she were always on the brink of being dumped.

When Molly thought of the little moments in which Louise dug into her confidence, she felt less bad about them by acknowledging that Molly had her own horribleness. Like Louise, she hadn't intended to be horrible, it just happened.

From behind the nail polish display, she watched Crystal for a moment. She must have been going to or coming from the gym because she'd never seen Crystal in leggings before. And her T-shirt was slightly cropped, revealing a strip of her low back. She had slight dimples on either side of her spine. Molly wanted to put her thumbs in those dimples and wrap her fingers around Crystal's hips. Instead, she turned around before Crystal retrieved her receipt. Molly found the single rolls of toilet paper and bought two, then a single roll of paper towel. She waited an extra minute before approaching the checkout to make sure Crystal had left. She looked at her watch, remembered it was worthless.

~

To her relief, The Human Bridge was still lying there when she returned. Molly said hello, and he said nothing. She set her purse in the office. She arranged the toilet paper and paper towel in the restroom, as though it were always there. This small victory had her body pumping full of adrenaline. She was ready to walk.

When she approached him, his face looked almost meditative. Molly took a deep breath and imagined walking across hot coals. She slipped off her shoes and cleared her throat. "I'm crossing the bridge now." She walked from his hips towards his shoulders.

He said nothing through the process. Didn't even groan. She stepped off from his chest onto the floor beside his ear. The bell atop the door chimed. Two women walked in. The older woman typed on her phone with one finger, and the younger woman trailed behind her. They didn't seem to notice The Human Bridge.

"This one, honey." The woman looked up from her phone and pointed to a painting. She turned to her daughter, "Wouldn't those leaves match perfectly with that new leather couch in the study?" They sounded like the most serious buyers Molly had witnessed so far. She stepped back into her shoes and approached them, leaving a few yards of space. She didn't want to crowd them.

There was movement in her periphery. The bridge was standing now. She watched him stretch, with his palms against his low back, and then walk out the door.

She hadn't the time to ponder him. The mother was already fishing in her purse for payment. The daughter took a photo of the painting with her phone.

Molly managed to use the card reader on the iPad to take their money in exchange for the painting. After she packaged the piece, the buyers left.

She looked at the bare spot on the wall, the bare spot on the floor. She turned on some music to fill the emptiness. She checked her phone. Louise had texted, asking how the gallery was going, what kind of stuff they were showing. *Good. Landscapes*, Molly replied. *Ew,* Louise responded immediately. Molly sat at the desk, returned the iPad to the drawer. She flipped to the next song on the streaming music station. Then she picked up her phone again. *They're pretty nice*. Molly sat and waited for someone else to come in.

The Dog

From: agerber@uda.edu
To: magicmichael4227@gmail.com
Subject: the dog

I want you to know that the dog is not dead and it's on its way to a full recovery.

But...

When I found it, the dog had been run over by a single Lexus SUV wheel. I was at the trails on Mount Fester (I've gotten more into hiking, on the suggestion of my new therapist, since our split). A car happened to be backing up as a woman happened to be walking her dog, and I happened to be exiting the trail. What are the odds of all this commotion on a Wednesday morning?

Seeing this dog, its body covered in a mantle of engine shadow, its brown paw twitching against the gravel, looking so much like Buster's paw when he slept, it brought me tender feelings towards our dog—your dog—Buster.

I remember the first inklings of wanting to leave you. At first it was this crazy idea buzzing past my mind like a fruit fly. How if I left you, I wouldn't have to deal with that damn dog any longer. He ate my face cream, entire bags of organic corn chips. Surely, you remember when he ate those capsules of CBD oil. I wondered, laughing, if he'd get high and have the munchies. "Too bad he already ate all the chips!" And then I saw you crying silently in that corner chair no one ever sits in, researching on your phone whether CBD was lethal to canines.

It was at that moment at the trailhead, when I reached under the car and felt wet fur, and then I pulled him into the daylight, that's when I missed Buster. I missed pushing him off our bed so I could have a place to sleep. I missed his terrible breath, a terrible that became comforting in its familiarity.

Just days before I asked to leave you (do you remember I asked permission? How funny sad things become later. How sad funny things become, too.) I went to Walmart.

I filled my cart with concealer, cereal, and a scarf. I wasn't paying attention to these first three things I'd grabbed. I was walking around the store like I was only half-awake. I was on my way to the Sports & Outdoors department. I couldn't stand the sight of blood, and I couldn't imagine leaving this earth with a stomachache or vomit on my face.

I wanted to shoot myself in the head. That's how it always happened in my mental movies, anyway. I passed through the aisles, among crossbows and ammunition. I got to the handguns, and my brain focused enough to register the model and price of one. An elderly man asked if I needed any assistance. I jumped—literally jumped. And I said no and scurried to the express checkout where I purchased what I later found out was concealer and cereal and a scarf.

I left these things in my trunk for a long time. I eventually ate the cereal. I didn't want it to go to waste. The concealer didn't match my skin tone. I gave the scarf to a coworker as a secret Santa gift.

Will you come back to me?

I can remember being a teenager, lying on the busted sofa in our basement with all the lights turned out, holding my hands at different positions (crossed like Dracula, down at my sides, clasped above my crotch), wondering how I'd be positioned in a casket. This is probably where I should have realized there was something wrong with me. Not just something wrong with my circumstances.

I have missed Buster more than I would have anticipated. Whenever I've run into your sister at the gym (Remember how my old therapist was always trying to get me to the gym?) my first question is always, "How's Buster?" Not just because I want to avoid asking about you right away, but also because he's the first thing I think of when I see her. This is probably because she was with us when we adopted him. Which is probably also why I always thought of him as your dog, because of the connection to your family. Is your sister still volunteering at the shelter? I always forget to ask her.

Maybe I don't really care whether she is or not. Maybe I just want to sit here longer in this memory of us in the pet supplies store five years ago. Remember how there was snow on the ground, even though it was April? During our first time walking him, he turned a spot yellow. And we laughed about the thought of picking up his little body to write our initials in the snow with his piss. Do you remember that? But he was (is) a small dog with a limited bladder, and we never tested the theory. The next time we walked him together the thought was no longer funny.

Do you think we could work if we tried again with fresh eyes?

Considering my hesitance around blood, it's amazing that I was brave enough to reach under the car and pull the dog out. (Though maybe, if I'm being honest, the thought of blood hadn't crossed my mind, and maybe if it had I wouldn't have been the one to reach under the car. Now that I consider it, I remember thinking, *wet*, upon touching it rather than *blood*.) I wasn't the bravest, just the first one to act in any productive way. The owner of the dog was crouched in a nearby pile of leaves, weeping and clutching her heart. The owner of the car was busy rifling in his glove compartment in an apparent state of shock, unable to recognize that he wouldn't need proof of insurance after vehicular homicide of a small animal. (Not *homicide*. Is there a word specific to murdering an animal? I'm afraid to look it up.) Cheryl (I found out later that the dog's owner was named Cheryl) took Arnie (this dog, a Jack Russell terrier) to the vet. Before she left, I asked for her phone number so I could get an update on the dog. I was invested now. Back in my own car, I wiped my fingers clean with a moist towelette, then dropped the pink-splotched disposable cloth into a plastic shopping bag. On the drive home, I convinced myself that if Arnie was okay it meant Buster was okay, but if Arnie was dead it meant something was really wrong with Buster (I kept imagining the phrase "inoperable tumor" in my head).

I called her when I got home. I dug my nails into my palms as the phone rang. I couldn't wait any longer to make sure he'd made it. As soon as I found out he was okay and could imagine Buster was okay, I started wondering if you were okay. And then I wondered if I was more okay when I was with you. I concluded that yes, I was, and that's why I turned on my computer and I started to write this to you.

Anyway, I hope you're well. I hope Buster is getting lots of chips.

—Me

Human Song

WE PULL OFF at the side of the highway in Somewhere, Maine. There's a deeper shoulder of gravel here, so we assume it to be a parking lot. The sky and the ocean and the rocks are all the same homesick color.

I remember how the bookshop owner had described it earlier, and I think, *Any place can be scenic, depending upon the scenes in your head.*

~

The used bookstore looked like many I'd visited in Detroit, filled with precarious stacks of yet-to-be-sorted volumes and uncomfortably narrow aisles. The culmination of too many histories gave me a headache. I understood the urge to reuse rather than throw away. But I couldn't imagine working in a place like this. Everyone's discarded things, the neediness of those artifacts, sapped me of my energy. The bookseller looked at home here, though. He leaned back in his office chair, and his khaki bucket hat blended into the raw wood shelving behind him. Without a word, Caleb disappeared into the poetry section in the back. I stayed by the front of the store and flipped through a collection of Hawthorne stories. The pages smelled like tobacco. The bookseller began asking me the questions he must have asked most obvious out-of-towners. *Where we were from* and *Where we were headed.* Caleb must have overheard and noted the opportunity to have a conversation with someone other than me. He emerged from the back sections. The bookseller nodded at him and said, "While you're here, you've gotta go sing to the snails." When he caught Caleb and I darting eyes as if they were magnetized to each other's, he clarified that the snails crept out of their shells when they heard human song. He said it was magical. Then, sensing our lack of imagination, he added that the spot was scenic. We were the most obvious of tourists, seeking scenery.

~

We walk onto the rocks towards the water. I'm wearing worthless sandals that slip off and keep finding places to get stuck. The whole trip Caleb's been pointing out my lack of adequate preparation. How I brought a backpack too small for my sleeping bag, so we've had to share one on our overnight hikes. It's new: his irritation with sharing. I reach out for Caleb's forearm to steady myself, but he hurries ahead. We crouch at a tide pool dotted with cochlear-shaped shells. He picks one up and starts singing Radiohead.

"It's too sad. No one would get out of bed for that," I say and take the shell into my own palm. I think about the kinds of songs that I listened to when I'd had enough of my own bleak monotony, when I grew tired of my own depression. I sing George Michael, then Spice Girls, then the Beatles.

"If they're not coming out for Ringo, there's nothing that'll do it," says Caleb. I've begun to feel this way about him, too. That nothing I can possibly do will bring him back to me. Caleb stands now, his knees cracking.

"We drove all this way and you're giving up already, huh?" I say.

"Let me know when you figure out what works." He walks to the shore.

I begin *Oohing, Ahhing*. Maybe the lyrics were what muddled the procedure. I try sonorous tones. Perhaps mimicking the sea might help. When I reach the notes that sound best against the wind, I see the snail's gray flesh wriggle. I shiver with minute satisfaction.

"It's working!"

Caleb returns, crouches back down, and looks closely. "Keep singing," he says.

I try changing my mouth's shape, adjusting pitch.

"It's not moving. You're seeing things." He stands and pulls a stone from his jacket pocket, attempts to skip it in the ocean. The surf reaches its hands towards the stone and pulls it in greedily. I set down the snail and reach for another, maybe one with different musical tastes.

When a Woman Walks Alone

WHEN A WOMAN walks alone she is asserting her independence. When a woman walks alone she is rebelling against fear. When a woman walks alone she can't help but think about what happens to women when they're alone.

Now, winding the path behind my neighborhood, between the river and the backyards, I think about Philip. He used to say hello. Shirtless, drinking from a mug on his porch when I first met him. He was one of the few neighbors who wanted to know my name, who invited me inside. I laughed in the way I do when I don't know what to say. Then I thought to say, "Thanks. Maybe some other time."

I like walking alone because I find no cause to laugh unless something is actually funny. I hear the cough of someone's HVAC unit turning on. The woods are so much thinner without the leaves. Anyone could see me through the nearly-bare limbs. Perhaps from their kitchen windows. I can't see them, so I don't think about them until their appliances communicate with me.

When I catch glimpses of people alone in their houses—when the sun is setting but inside the lights are on and it doesn't seem dark enough yet to draw the curtains—it depresses me. Everyone's aloneness depresses me because it reflects my own. The wind blows harder. The surface of the water ripples, and I watch one just-fallen leaf blow across it in the opposite direction of the river flow. I could make it into a superficial metaphor.

I keep walking and tell myself not to think about severed limbs.

My hound would have alerted me if he were still alive, walking with me in these woods. Jeb loved discovering disgusting things invisible to the human eye or nose. I was walking him when the police descended. Two SUVs with *Forensic Unit* painted across their sides. The lights weren't on, but we could feel the hum of activity. Jeb nosed his way under a nearby walnut tree and found a stray turd to nibble on before I could yank him away. My neighbor walked by with her miniature greyhound. Out of habit I held open my palm for his tiny tongue to lick. I asked my neighbor if she knew what was going on. "They're searching Philip's house. That missing woman—you've seen the flyers—she was a friend of his."

~

I love the crunch of dried leaves beneath my feet. The late afternoon sun filters through the tangle of branches and skitters across the water. I turn around to feel it on my face, but the wind blows away the warmth before it can land on my cheeks. Behind me I think I hear footsteps. I turn and see no one. It was a squirrel, I'm sure. Their sounds become amplified when I'm alone. Every small animal is bigger, more threatening, without Jeb around. I turn back and focus on what's ahead. I try to enjoy myself. This free time, this nature. My next step rolls forward on something, and I almost fall. I look down and expect to see a finger. It's only a twig.

She was left in these woods in pieces. She was a friend of his. Perhaps if she'd been walking alone she would have been safer. *I'm safe*, I say to myself.

Trees have been falling lately. Maybe they always do, and I just notice them more now, walking alone. One great oak stretches across the river; its roots dense like a loofah at the opposite shore. I suddenly want to hug the tree standing beside me. I think of the people washing dishes at their windows and lean a hand against its bark instead.

Up ahead I notice a bright spot among the brown. As I come closer, I see it's one white sock. I inspect it to make sure it's empty. It has been turned inside out, the way I leave mine when I'm too tired, flicking my clothes off after work. I can see a round darkened patch where a big toe has made its imprint. It's one of those low-cut socks they started making when exposed sock became unfashionable.

A woman was here. A woman running. Maybe this fell from her pocket, or it was stuck in the leg of her athletic pants, which she'd been wearing another time before washing. I imagine her with headphones on. She's a newer resident, unaware of last year's local news. She has a position at the nearby university. She is self-motivated, the way runners are, the type who does not have time to think about all the ways she can be murdered. And maybe that's my real problem, I think. I have too much time to think.

Then there's a real woman coming towards me, and I stop thinking of the imagined one. I recognize her, this neighbor who speaks to her little white dog but never to me, not even when I say hello and try to make eye contact in passing. Again I say hello, and again she says nothing, just pulls her little dog away from the brush off the trail and scolds him by clicking tongue against teeth. Perhaps not speaking to strangers is her way of coping when she is walking alone.

With Gun

AFTER WORK, I went for a walk with a colleague who is blind. I drove as he directed me to a nature trail. He said he had once ridden his bike on it. I was learning all sorts of obvious things, like that the visually impaired could also ride bikes.

It was early autumn. There were a few leaves on the ground. He slid his cane along the path. I warned him of the changes in terrain, the wooden footbridge, the swamp. I noticed flowers I'd never seen grow near my apartment. I felt a bud of guilt at the center of my joy.

We hadn't previously spent time together outside of work, though we were classroom neighbors, both in our thirties. We chatted daily, sharing anecdotes about our young children. We were both looking for something to do between the school day and parent-teacher conferences. I was preserving my stores of sociability and didn't feel like talking much. I admired the scenery instead.

"My biggest fear on these trails is that I'll come across teenagers smoking weed," he said, breaking the silence. I asked why that frightened him. "I wouldn't want to get them in trouble." We were both teachers of teenagers, so it seemed an odd statement. "You wouldn't have to do anything," I said. He ignored my comment. I was used to my students ignoring me, so I didn't take it too personally.

"I'd rather come across a man with a gun," he said. I made a confused exclamation. "Then, at least, I'd know what to do," he clarified. I wondered if the real reason was that he couldn't see the gun, but he could smell the marijuana. Maybe it wasn't that he would know what to do with a man with a gun, but that he wouldn't know about the gun at all. I said nothing, though. I felt uncomfortable acknowledging his blindness. And it occurred to me that I'm more at ease, myself, confronting what I cannot see.

At the end of the trail was a small lake. He asked me the direction of the water flow. I described the ripples. He took a selfie and posted it to Twitter, Snapchat. I stood outside the frame.

He asked if the leaves had turned yet. I identified small patches of orange. "Mostly it's still green," I said. "That's what I thought," he answered.

After Leaving

THERE'S A SURRENDER and ease in being told what to do. It was something I never would have anticipated missing after leaving him.

Once I've settled in at the Best Western, I think of calling my sister, Astrid. I'd hate to disturb her, though. She's recently given birth to twins. I don't want to burden her. I'll wait to talk until she asks me for help, I think. She may want a babysitter soon.

I decide I'll take myself out for dinner. It's been so many months since I've been out to a restaurant. Date nights dwindled after the early stage of our relationship. I suspect he didn't feel proud of me anymore, didn't feel I was worth showing off or spending money on.

~

Downtown, the trees lining the streets are turning orange. There's a sweet scent of decay in the air. I've always liked autumn best. He used to say it's because I'm a melancholy woman. The same reason I find sad songs the most beautiful.

There are too many options: Thai, Vietnamese, French, that cafe with ten types of soup. I step towards a bar and grill, read the menu in the window. I step away, arrested by doubt. My throat starts to tighten and my chest caves in. I do the same with the pizza place. Inside, people sit at the counter along the window. There's no other seating. I think I'll feel too exposed, like an animal in a zoo exhibit. I walk away and sit on a bench. I take deep breaths. I tell myself, *There's no wrong answer! Just pick!*

I choose Tavola, an Italian restaurant I've always wanted to try. Inside, the decor is impeccable, the scent divine. Garlic and herbs and yeasty bread. But the noise is overwhelming. The tables too small and close. They're all filled with friends or lovers or families.

A stylishly dressed couple gets up to leave. They look at me as they pass, the lonely patron waiting to request a table for one. My insides contract further. He liked to say I fear people, that it's best I just stay home.

It was true, I feared the infinite possible judgments of strangers. At least his I could anticipate.

My girl, what would you do without me taking care of you?

When the hostess arrives, I panic and ask to place an order of fettuccine alfredo to go. I sit down at the chair by the door and scroll through unsettling headlines on my phone.

At the park, I find a picnic table by the river and eat my fine meal with plastic utensils. It was too expensive. I should have just picked up a sandwich from the gas station. It seems every decision I make is the wrong one. I wonder whether I should have just stayed.

I venture toward the paved trail, as though I can walk away from the thought. And it works to some degree, as physical movement often does, shaking loose whatever mental loop I might be trapped in.

The sounds of the river always calm me. The moving water gives off a slight breeze. I pass several dogs with their owners. Their grateful snouts make me feel happy for a moment. My phone rings. I need to change the ringtone because its familiar sound makes my chest hurt. On the screen, it's not his name, so I can breathe again. It's my neighbor, Ciely. She says her internet is out again and she doesn't know why. I tell her I can be there in thirty minutes, and I turn around to head back to my truck.

~

I like visiting Ciely. I like her softened old couches covered in dog hair, the collection of frog figurines on every available surface. I like helping her with technology, with walking her dog. She says she's too old to walk Harrold as much as she should. She's too exhausted. Visiting my neighbor was one of the rare places I could go without all the constant texts and phone calls to check in on me, without him grilling me about who I saw and where I went after I got home.

"What's wrong?" Ciely says, her face concerned but voice void of pity, when she opens her front door. She has a matter-of-fact way of talking that I find comforting. Especially when I don't want to feel what I'm trying not to feel.

"Taz and I broke up."

After a moment of staring at me, she says, "Welp, you'll find someone else."

I nod and go to the router by the mantle, which is covered in framed photos of her children, now grown. I can't help but think, *You never did.*

I tell her I found a cheap basement apartment just outside of town, where I can move in on the first of the month. The new landlord, who lives on the top floor and spends most of his time on the porch, gives me the creeps. My reluctance to walk by him when I go out matters little. I'll feel safer inside my new home, and that's got to be more important.

My phone rings. It's Astrid. Ceily tells me to take it, but I silence the ringer and let it go to voicemail.

I ask her how to live alone. It feels okay with Ciely to admit I've never done it before.

"You need routines. And a pet. A dog is great because they've got the routines built right in." She picks up Harrold and scratches his head, like she's just remembered he's sitting dutifully beside her. "They'll get you out of the house for walks. Good if you're a bit of a hermit like me." She gives me a knowing look and sets Harrold down.

"You're still young and pretty, so you should get a big, scary dog."

I picture myself with a pit bull. It occurs to me this is perhaps the same reason I chose a Silverado when the Civic lease ended. Little props might earn you some distance when you're a woman, when everyone feels entitled to your space.

I troubleshoot the internet, unplugging and plugging back in the router. It's working now. It just so happens I can do things on my own.

She thanks me, sends me home with some recently expired Tylenol she's acquired from a hoarder friend. "Whenever I visit her house, I put a few things in my purse when she's not looking. It helps her out."

For all the times I've come over here, we've never touched. I ask her for a hug and she says, in a tone that's almost scolding, "Of course!"

I try not to cry with my face resting on her shoulder. I hold my eyes tight and bite my lip. When I pull away, I look at her, and her mouth makes a faint line of sympathy.

"Welp, I'm sure you have lots to do." She grabs my forearm with one hand and taps my wrist with another. "You'll be okay."

~

There's cable in the hotel room. Still, I end up on ABC, where the new season of The Bachelorette is airing. I linger here, feel a bloom of shame, then flip the channel to PBS. I flip back, remembering Taz saying reality TV is fake, it's for idiots. But he's not here, and his opinions are not facts. There's a flutter in my chest when it comes back on, this pink-faced woman before so much possibility.

My body has warmed the sheets overnight, and they release the scent of bulk detergent. The light comes through the sheer polyester curtains and illuminates the empty hotel walls. Sometimes I wake up so lonely I feel like I might spontaneously combust. Too much nothing. I think resentment feels better than nothing.

Then I think, *This nothing will eventually be filled with something better.*

Easier to Convince

"Do you shop at Walmart?" It's the first thing Paula asks once we're parked and she's turned toward me, sitting in the backseat. I laugh for a second. *Is this a test? A joke?* But her eyes are earnest. She smiles and a crooked incisor pushes against her upper lip, so just the right side shows a gleam of ivory splitting the soft seal of her mouth.

"Um, I've been there before."

"I thought I recognized your skirt. I have one like that in green, a wrap-around?" She leans toward me from the passenger seat. Paula reaches to lift the edge of my shirt, revealing a tie at my waist. "Yeah, like this one. Is that where you got it?"

I pull back until the hem of my shirt is freed from her grip and smooth the linen draped over my lap. "I think I got this at a swap meet."

She keeps talking, first about swap meets, then monologuing about thrift stores and how she never finds anything good at the ones up here. She combs her light brown hair out of her face with her fingers. Paula's glasses look old, out of style. But she behaves as though everything about her is sexy, so even the warped brown frames are, too.

I'd heard lots about Maggie's "up-north best friend" Paula. Maggie and her professor parents spent each summer at their lake house in the small town where Paula lived year-round. They forged the kind of unlikely friendship that only endures when it's built on shared childhood memories. I'm sure Paula has heard a lot about me too, the "downstate best friend." In spite of this and sharing a best friend, I still feel she's acting too familiar with me.

Maggie finally comes back to the car, having found the magic mushrooms and her "she wee," a funnel-like contraption she received as a gag gift but has since touted for the way it levels the outdoor urination playing field. We are headed to the Summer Solstice Gathering, a small music festival on a farm in northern Michigan, which Maggie and I have gone to for the past three years. This is the last one we'll have together before we split paths for college, or wherever.

As the hour-long drive from Maggie's lake house to the farm wears on, Paula's and Maggie's voices lower, and they engage in a conversation that inevitably leaves out the person in the backseat. From what bits I can hear, Maggie is rehashing her plans for a gap year before college. She has a lot of ideas about her future. Though she's been accepted into the University of Michigan, Kalamazoo, and State, she keeps talking about a year abroad. I can't imagine putting such opportunities on hold. Maggie, though, has a way about her that makes anything seem like a good idea. I look out the window at the passing fields, the goldenrod and purple loosestrife waving along the edge of the highway like watercolor paint strokes. I leave them to catch up on their time apart. I think of Damien instead, of what I might say when I see him again.

~

Maggie had been up north for spring break when Damien and I met, so she hadn't witnessed our intense connection. Had she, she wouldn't have been so quick to tease me for stalking him online. As Maggie walked the beach and read every Murakami novel, I worked at a café. A job I romanticized for the first few days and resented once I realized it was all about kissing ass and cleaning filth.

The café had a small stage and a weekly open mic, at which the same cast of locals bought the cheapest drip coffee on the menu and tipped little to none to sit around for two hours until it was their turn to strum the ukulele and sing-cry about love, or whatever. But every now and then we got a real band to perform. Like the Friday before spring break ended. In what I justify as a karmic gift from the universe to make up for my otherwise horrible vacation, in came a banjo-playing man with dark curls that grazed his shoulders and a lip ring I was determined to bite. From the register I could watch as he played with eyes closed, nearly making out with the microphone. The entire situation was cliché, I knew, but I was transfixed. I felt high watching him play. And the music was good too. He was accompanied by an older woman on cello, with non-threatening salt and pepper hair, and a drummer who smiled too wide and goofy for a percussionist, even one in a folk band.

After their set, I tracked his movements while I wiped down the espresso machine. A puddle of milk dripped onto my foot. I crouched down to wipe the toe of my sneaker. Upon standing, I found Damien in front of me. Instead of telling him we were closed, like I had the last straggling groupie before him, I asked what sounded good.

"Any recommendations, Alex?" He looked at my name tag, and the sound of my name in his mouth made my heart flutter. His speaking voice was much gravellier than his singing voice.

I made my recent favorite concoction, an iced earl grey tea shaken with cream, rosewater, and cardamom syrup. I made one for myself in the chipped mug I designated for my shift drink. When he got out his wallet I waved it off. "On the house."

He lingered at the counter as he took the first sip. I grabbed mine and took a sip alongside him. It was silly, but for a moment I blushed, imagining I was on a date with this guy rather than serving him. He made a face and shook his head, his curls bouncing.

My blushing cheeks turned full-on scorching. "Not for you?" I asked, trying to sound nonchalant rather than mortified.

"Tastes a little perfume-y." He laughed and apologized for his unsophisticated palate.

"Not everyone's a fan of floral drinks."

He pulled a flask from his jacket and added a pour of brown liquor, then held it out to me. I shrugged and said, "Sure." As he doctored my drink, his bandmates called goodnight and he gave them a brief acknowledgement over his shoulder. There seemed to be a mutual understanding among them about cockblocking.

I'd never been so happy to be the one closing. I locked the doors as he settled into the wilting leather couch. I'd given him free reign of the old iPod that controlled the café's soundtrack, and he'd chosen Rufus Wainwright. I withheld any praise for his musical taste. Damien might have had some years on me, but I knew how to play the game with a guy like him, for whom music is the life raft to which his ego clings. I set a bottle of Riesling and a couple glasses at the table, then sat down on the other end of the couch. I made a mental note to pay for the wine before leaving. I was breaking a number of rules, sure, but the only ones Cheryl and David, the owners, really cared about involved the till.

We drank the wine. I shifted my body awkwardly until I found a comfortable enough position angled toward him, my leg an inch away from his. He gazed at the menu board as he recounted the history of his band, The Talismans. I watched the silver hoop on his lower lip rise and fall and half-followed what he said. He turned to me and smiled when he was done talking. I took the cue and managed to say "Cool," in return, which was apparently a satisfactory enough answer because he set down his drink and leaned toward me. I straightened up, arched my back, and he scooped his arm behind me, as though this were choreographed. One thing I like about older guys is they don't let the preemptive conversation go on too long. First kisses with teenagers always seemed to happen after a series of maddening baby steps. The inching of fingers, the incremental leaning toward one another. So many hormones yet so much doubt of reciprocity. A fish swimming in water doesn't know what water is, or however the saying goes.

We spent nearly an hour making out on the couch. I luxuriated in the feeling of getting exactly what I wanted. I nibbled his lip ring until he pulled back just enough to whisper, "Careful." I shifted attention to his lips and tongue. Then we took a walk around the block as he smoked, eventually returning to the café, where Damien retrieved his banjo and said he wanted to show me something. I followed him to a powder blue van in the parking lot. He slid open the door to reveal a narrow bed, yellow floral curtains, and a southwestern patterned rug. He had a potted succulent affixed to the wall below the window. I was charmed by the way he'd nested in his traveling home. With one foot resting in the doorway he slid his banjo under the bed, then turned to me and grabbed my hand. "Come in?"

I looked back at the café, at my car in the employee spot. I surveyed the parking lot which had gone from packed to deserted since I'd last been here. I squeezed his hand and kissed him one last time. "I better not."

It felt good to walk away like that, like I left with some power still intact, which didn't always feel the case. Of course, on my way home I was furious at myself for not getting Damien's number. Maybe he didn't want it anyway. Musicians didn't look back. He had a *fuck van,* for god's sake. Still, I thought of him for weeks. And when I saw The Talismans on the Summer Solstice Gathering lineup, my obsession was reinforced by the promise of seeing him again.

~

There is a line half a mile down the dirt road from the festival gates. Staff members in orange vests check tickets and IDs and affix wristbands. Each year, it gets bigger, more professional, and a little less quaint. I feel anxious at the sight of the hundreds of cars parked in the fields. Eventually, we find a spot to park and a place to pitch our tent. Paula takes charge. Out of the passenger seat, she has more of a presence now. She doesn't have the same hunched-over posture my classmates do, which I assume is from a mixture of phone addiction and insecurity. It strikes me at this moment that I haven't once seen Paula pull out a phone. Maybe she doesn't even have one.

After our campsite is set up, I request that we smoke a bowl before going to the action. I need a moment to shift my mindset, to become Fun Alex. As we walk the dirt trail to the section where RVs are parked, I'm surprised by how many people Paula knows. She'd been busy working and unable to join in past years, so I'd assumed Maggie and I would be leading the charge at the festival, with Paula as our sort of rookie underling.

"Damn, there's a lot more vendors here this year," says Maggie, looking around and fixing her hair. Her pixie cut is currently tinged blue, but it's been nearly every color over the course of high school. She's barely over five feet, with the pep of two people combined. I wonder if her compact body conserves energy better.

"Yeah, remember when it was just the farm kitchen and the smoothie truck guy?" I'm nostalgic for that time. Why is it that I feel so protective of what's special to me, even when it can't be taken away? Sharing an experience with a greater number of people shouldn't make it less special, but it somehow carves out some emptiness at its center, makes it feel hollow.

"Sam Sam the smoothie man?" Paula says with a skip. "Oh yeah, that's him," she points to a purple truck.

"You know that guy?" says Maggie.

Paula steps in front of us and raises her eyebrows. "Oh, I *know him*."

"Ew, he's like forty!" Maggie says and gets out a cigarette. People are pushing past us on the narrow path, so we step aside while she lights it.

Over the course of the weekend I would learn details about Paula that Maggie had left out. Paula lived in a town with a population just shy of 500 and hadn't been to school since the sixth grade. She was a year younger than me, seventeen, but she carried herself like an adult. Probably because everyone in her world – parents, siblings, niece, coworkers – had been treating her as one since she was thirteen, the year she started working full time (or "homeschooling," if the state of Michigan asked, but they rarely asked). Paula's reality was so different from my own. Where I thought rural life would have sheltered her, it had made her grow up quickly.

Everywhere we walk, I think Damien is about to appear. We do a lap around the vendors, the barn stage, and the large main stage. We lay in the grass adjacent to the small outdoor stage where a bluegrass band is playing. I feel my muscles relax for the first time in a while. The way you don't realize you're tensing until you have a chance to consciously release always astonishes me. Paula passes me a spliff and I suck on it before learning what's inside. I melt further and the grass tickles my neck. Soon, the music feels obnoxiously repetitive, each song essentially the same. I sit up and propose we find something more danceable. Really, I'm impatient to see him. Maggie is braiding Paula's hair. "In a minute," she says in a way that I know means ten or twenty. I say I'll catch them later and trudge on. Now that we've arrived, it feels apparent we're here for different purposes.

I cut through the woods to the main stage, stepping around brush and makeshift campsites.

And then I see him.

Not Damien. The *him* I never want to see. And my breath is immediately suctioned into nowhere. My heart starts racing. I can prepare for this when I'm going to the required family functions. But I wasn't expecting to see him here. Tyler is starting a small fire in front of a tarp canopied over several camping chairs. Even in a tie dye shirt, he doesn't look like he fits in here. Before he can look up from the kindling, I run. It's a feeling I couldn't explain if I wanted to. Sometimes when I see my cousin, I'm okay. I can focus on whoever else I'm talking to at the party or funeral. I can ignore him like he's merely a character in a TV show that's playing in the background. Other times, I become consumed with anger. I visualize picking up a nearby utensil and stabbing him with it. I wish for a shovel to bash his head in. I try to breathe. I go into the bathroom. I hyperventilate and try to steady my vitals. I splash cold water on my face. Here, though, there's only more trees, a row of porta-potties. Once I've gained enough distance, I find a large trunk to lean against. I tell myself I'm being insane. This is not a logical reaction. What he did to me was not that bad. It was years ago. Why is the sight of him making me terrified? I touch the bark of the tree I'm resting on. I find three things I can feel, see, hear, like that video said to do. I tell myself I'm safe.

A group of non-threatening hippies walk by. "You okay, sis?" says a woman with purple-stained teeth. She reaches down and helps me up. I want to collapse into her arms, nuzzle my face in her white girl dreadlocks. Instead I offer her some weed in return and we smoke, her friends standing at a polite distance but waiting up. I follow them to the main stage and soon I'm blended into a crowd of moving bodies, familiar in the way spectators at a concert look vaguely similar, all seemingly related by only one or two degrees of separation.

I go to find water. I realize I didn't bring my purse or cash; it's all in Maggie's car. There's a fire pit nearby where a drum circle is underway. I spot a big red cooler and plan to make friends. The sun is readying to tuck behind the tree line. I shield my eyes and sit on an empty stump, waiting for my heart to slow. All the drummers are men, the women hang nearby watching and listening, in a scene that looks much more antiquated than progressive. The guy with the cooler introduces himself as Child Flower. The name gives me a slight shiver but I accept the can of iced tea he offers. He smiles at me too long, until a young girl pulls him away. I close my eyes and take long sips. I realize I'm incredibly high. I try to extinguish Tyler from my mind. I remember the festivals of earlier years and remember I am here. I am safe.

"Alex!" I flinch and open my eyes. There's an arm around my middle. It's Maggie. Thank god. She and Paula have plates of food. An extra shawarma for me. I think I could cry tears of gratitude when I accept the food, accept their company. With Child Flower gone, they sit on his stump and the unattended cooler. As they chew, I notice the smoothness of their foreheads, their bobbing jawlines. Maggie has sauce on her chin and I'd tease her about it but I'm too hungry to stop eating my sandwich. The drumming slows and finally dissipates, the real music now audible from a distance. We finish our dinners, and they do not question my demeanor or where I've been. Another mercy.

Now that the sun has set, so have the acoustics. Electric guitars and keyboards take their place. In the barn, there are multicolored lights flashing, an upgrade in technology since last year. We're dancing and drinking rum, courtesy of Paula, who has quickly earned my acceptance. My thoughts have slowed to a delicious pace. I'm not thinking of him. I'm not even thinking of Damien. My body feels paradoxically warm and numb with the movement. Then I see dark curls bouncing in the crowd. I've been deceived before. But the curls move closer and people part until his face is visible too.

"Hey!" I shout and point at him.

Damien's searching face turns to recognition and he points back.

"Hey, I know that lip ring!" I yell over the electric fiddle solo.

"You do!" He laughs and snakes a hand around my waist in a side hug.

"Where've you been?" I ask. Sometimes I don't know how drunk I am until I hear what I'm blurting out.

"I just got here," his hot breath says in my ear. He grabs my hand and twirls me around. When he pulls me back to him we dance the way my grandparents used to dance at weddings. I find it charming, how nerdy he can be, which is what happens when someone so attractive acts so corny. I want him to kiss me, but he doesn't. I want to pick up where we left off, but it occurs to me maybe he's with someone. A lot can change in a few months. Hell, maybe he was with someone then, too.

"Are you thirsty?" he asks after the song ends and we stop dancing to catch our breath. I say yes and follow him out of the barn. It's pitch dark now. Beyond the fire pit, beyond the other stages, the lights dwindle. A few flashlights bobbing and lamps glowing. We walk the trail and then through rows of cars. He says he has beers in his van. Both the quiet and the cold sneak up on me. I'm bracing myself, expecting to see *him* again. Damien is moving quickly and I have to jog for a few paces to catch up.

"Here we are," he says. The sound of the door sliding open is somehow more familiar than it should be. I think of déjà vu. I think of premonitions. I think I'm probably wasted.

This time, I follow him inside. There's just enough

room for us both to sit cross legged, facing one another. He pulls out a couple beers from somewhere and uncaps them on a bottle opener affixed to the wall next to the succulents. With a satisfied smile, he hands me one, foaming over. I suck it down and he watches me lick the remaining foam off the glass.

We sit in silence, looking at each other for a few moments. He's installed several of those "As Seen on TV" Taplights to the interior of the van. The one overhead illuminates his bloodshot eyes. He says it's great to see me again, asks if I knew he'd be here. Instead of answering, I lean in to kiss him. My movements are constrained by the storage tub behind me, the metal frame of his makeshift bed hitting my knee. I don't know where to set my beer so I hold it up behind his back, hoping it won't spill. When he notices my struggle, he takes both of our drinks and tucks them into cupholders, hidden on the other side of the bedspread. He puts his cold hands under my shirt. I feel the heat leach from my abdomen into his palms and fingers. He moans and gets up to come closer to me, hitting his head on the ceiling in the process. With an effortful grunt he lifts me onto the bed and slides on top of me. I don't know where my own limbs are anymore. His hands are running up my legs now, fingers grazing the creases between my thighs and crotch. My body seizes, stays frozen.

He lifts his chin from my neck. "Are you okay?"

It takes me a while to form my response. He pushes up from the cot onto his forearms, and the frame beneath us creaks. "What is it?"

My face is curtained by his hair, in the kind of frame I'd fantasized about during the past weeks since I'd met him. In my imaginings, there was more air around us. It wasn't all so confined and stifling.

"I'm—uh, on my moon time," I lie.

He looks puzzled, and I'm not sure if it's because he's mature enough to be okay with that or because I've been too subtle.

"I'd prefer to not do this while I'm on my period, ya know?"

He chuckles and nods too vigorously, sits up and grabs his beer again. He holds it in both hands and takes a long drink. I can almost imagine him as a little boy, doing the same with a bottle of Sunny-D.

I leave the van with a half-formed excuse he agrees to before I've finished the sentence. I slide on my sandals, toes on one foot misplaced. But I'm unable to stop to adjust the flip flop before stalking off into the night. There are so many cars here, so many distant voices, stoned laughter, drunken guffawing. I keep walking, back into the light and sound pollution. Back to some feeling of safety, I hope.

The bonfire is surging. Some pyro no doubt got carried away in drunken flame worship. I need to sit, re-stabilize. I ask a bearded man in a crocheted vest to scoot over and make room for me on the log. I fix my shoes and wipe the tears from my face. Paula and Maggie are nowhere in sight. A craggy hand holds out a pill. I look up at the man and ask him what it is.

"A vitamin." Light dances in the reflection of his dark irises.

My body says *danger*. But I don't want to be here anymore, so I take the capsule. The cooler is nearby, and I open it, fish out an ice cube and let it melt on my tongue. The pill slides down with the dripping water.

As I sit and wait for something to happen, I imagine

Paula and Maggie know to find me here, where they found me before. I tell myself this is our psychically agreed-upon meeting place. My mind has always been easily manipulated, but the drugs make it even easier to convince myself of anything. I tell myself I'm having a good time. Soon, there's a drum between my knees and I'm beating it. The feeling is good. It makes sense. I'm a part of something here, and it's both collaborative and destructive.

~

The time has come. I can't hold it anymore. It's inevitable here, yet I always try to avoid it as long as possible. I have to use the porta-potty. I select the one on the far end, hoping it's the least abused. The door flings open easily, and with it a blast of toilet mint and fecal fragrance. It's dark, and I'm grateful I can't see what's below me. Rather than sit, I lean forward and lift my long skirt, assume a squatting position, hovering over the toilet. Once it starts to flow, spigot-like, I can't stop it, but I know something's not right. My calves are wet, then my ankles. I feel it trickle down to my feet. My eyes have had time to adjust now, and I look between my legs at the toilet seat cover, which is down. It's covered in pee, and so are my legs, my skirt, the floor.

I'm too disoriented for cleanup, but I lift the lid of the toilet as a precaution for the next person. I dash out towards the campsite. Immediately my legs are cold and itchy against the night air. I look for the Tibetan prayer flags that were strung up in the trees beside our tent. There are small light sources here and there. Between them I keep my hands out in front of me to feel for obstructions. I can't remember where I saw Tyler, so I can't remember where to avoid. I tell myself he doesn't know I'm here so he won't be looking for me, won't notice me if I walk by, a stumbling figure in the dark.

When I reach the tent, it is illuminated, a glowing blue haven. I see their outlines, hear their voices as I approach. When I unzip the door and crawl in, I'm overcome with relief.

"Dude, you stink," says Maggie, in lieu of a greeting.

I remember and recount the porta-potty incident. Paula bursts into laughter, a sort of neighing guffaw that is so ungraceful I think I'm in love. Maggie switches into her caretaker mode, though. She's usually the one to take on the role of den mother when a friend is too inebriated, a trait that I have always admired, but especially now, when I am the piss-soaked child. She wipes down my legs with wet wipes and throws them into a bag. She holds it out to me, and I realize she's asking for my skirt, which I can finally see in the light of the lantern is spattered and a quarter drenched. I unwrap it from my waist, ball it up, and put it in the bag. Maggie ties the bag tight and tosses it outside. She emits a sigh. "Better."

We pass around a gas station Gatorade and bag of corn chips. I listen to each recount the evenings' absurdities. I pull on my pajama pants and then a blanket. Soon all three of us are underneath, spooning. I feel safe. I tell them I love them and fall asleep.

~

I wake up earlier than I wish to. The quiet, though, is welcome. After staring at the condensation on the tent walls for some time, failing to fall back asleep, I get up and attempt to leave the tent with as little disturbance as possible. Maggie is snoring gently. Paula twitches and rubs her nose at the sound of my stirring but does not wake. Outside, birds are making their presence known. I pull up my hood on my sweatshirt and put on my sunglasses, the disguise of celebrities getting their groceries. A couple chipmunks are pawing at a bag of corn nuts, and a finch lands nearby, looking for crumbs. I'd been so excited to party with like-minded music lovers. Now, walking the narrow trail, past endless beer cans and cigarette butts, I feel disgusted with my species. It's not so uncommon, I remind myself, this feeling of having anticipated a getaway only to arrive and start counting down the hours until I can go home.

I head towards the festival epicenter in search of coffee. There's a large shed converted into a kitchen near the barn, where the radio sounds of Heart's "Crazy on You" waft out. A woman sings along, then breaks into a smoker's cough.

I approach the open window where she is washing dishes and greet her good morning. It takes her a moment to realize I'm speaking to her. "Morning, hon. Need something to do?" I hear voices behind her asking if it's Rita. The woman at the window turns to the other ladies and says that Rita is "sick," using air quotes with her intonation. She turns back to me and offers free meals in exchange for a few hours in the kitchen.

Inside, the sound of clattering pans is amplified. The feeling among the group of three women reminds me of my aunts in the kitchen during a holiday party. Sue is seemingly the leader. She wipes sweat from her forehead with a hot pink bandanna and asks me to take over chopping apples. It's nice to have a task to distract me. The apples are small and come in odd shapes, like they've just been gathered from the ground on the property, which

I figure they probably have. We are making a gigantic pot of oats, pans of scrambled eggs and red skin potatoes, and Ellen is in charge of a miraculous set of Dutch babies in cast iron skillets. The smells inside are comforting, as is the feeling of being productive rather than purely hedonistic. Ellen asks me where I'm from, and I learn her daughter lives in Ann Arbor, too. I want to ask her more but she turns around and begins setting up the tables of food lined outside the kitchen building. In years past, to save money, I always brought my own food, but I envied those with hot meals from the farm's kitchen.

As directed, I cook down the chopped apples with butter, brown sugar, cinnamon, and nutmeg. I want to dive into the skillet and swim inside.

"Beautiful!" Sue proclaims in her scratchy voice, her long gray hair nearly dipping into the fruit as she leans over the burner. I warm under her appreciation. One of the things I'll miss about being a kid, I think, is impressing adults with my self-reliance. The praise dwindles as I get older. When we're finished cooking, I stand at the front of the row of tables and take meal tickets. Sue tells me to pocket four of them to redeem later. It seems the campers have awoken. A line snakes around the hand washing station and behind the barn.

Once the line shortens, Ellen gives me a hug and tells me to go. "Have fun, kid." I carry a plate heaped with everything to the picnic tables, scanning to make sure there are no signs of him. I find an open spot. Here I can look into the trees and beyond, where the property ends with yellow tape and signs of warning.

It doesn't occur to me to feel left out until I see them walking toward me, a pair of best friends starting their day together. I offer them two of my remaining tickets and wait for their return.

Paula and Maggie join me with their breakfasts. Maggie unveils her bag of dried mushrooms and adds a few caps to her eggs, then passes them to Paula, who does the same. I hate to ruin the taste in my mouth, but I toss one back and chew, then wash it down with coffee. This had been the plan: on Saturday we trip. Maggie is quiet in the mornings and I'm feeling introverted, so Paula carries the conversation. She opens her festival program on the table and proposes our plan for which acts to catch over the course of the day. "Oh, we can see Indigo at two."

"But that's when Alex's boyfriend is playing!" Maggie interjects with a playground-chant tone to her voice on the word "boyfriend."

I roll my eyes and smile but don't protest. I don't feel like talking about last night. Thankfully, they don't ask me. I roll my neck, then stand up and do some stretches. In pain from sleeping on the ground, I look forward to losing some awareness of my body.

~

We listen to a band only Paula knows of, and then a young mandolin player Maggie met at a summer camp back in middle school. Each time we change locations I put on my sunglasses and hood and survey the area for signs of him. Once I'm feeling safe, I can settle in. Onstage is the newly-married folk duo who own the farm. Their love songs make my chest swell. When Keaton sings a new song to Rosie Lee and she starts to cry, I tear up too. Paula is sitting next to me, her patchwork skirt splayed out inches away. When she notices me wiping my eyes she holds out her hand. I take it.

Fingers still entwined with Paula's, I lay back in the

grass and feel the sun on my face. I'm waiting for the mushrooms to kick in. Paula points out the movement of the leaves in a way that tells me she's feeling the effects. Maggie, after a long story about how she taught the mandolin player to use a tampon, gets suddenly quiet again. That's how I know she's feeling it too. I open my eyes to a curtain of light. Onstage, there's movement but minimal sound. A few saws of the cello, a banjo being tuned, the crash of a fallen cymbal. I sit up, cross-legged, and pull grass from the ground in front of my feet. Maggie is holding a dandelion under her chin and asking me if she likes butter. I give her a shove and tell her to play with my hair. Paula has gone to find someone with a spare cigarette. When Damien introduces the band, Maggie squeezes my shoulder. I tap my head to signal her to return to raking my scalp with her fingers. We are close enough to see him clearly, but – I hope – far enough that I don't appear like a desperate fan, that I don't stand out in the crowd. Suddenly, everyone's movements appear fast and jerky. Damien bobbles his head as he plucks at his banjo and romances the microphone. The group of girls next to us hoot and holler, then get up and dance. Damien grins at them. I try to remember him in the café. Was he the same then as now? He appears so showy and desperate, as he stomps his foot alongside the bass drum beats, in a move so clearly practiced. It all feels planned and pathetic. I get up and find Paula, who is talking with a couple biker dudes in skull caps and leather vests under the shade of a nearby tree. I ask to bum a smoke and listen to them discuss Kurt Vonnegut. I almost express my surprise to learn that Paula has read his books—she'd told me last night about leaving school. But the men jump in quickly and I, thankfully, miss my opportunity to accidentally insult her. I turn back to watch the stage. They're playing a song I've listened to dozens of times on their Bandcamp site. The words "whispering insincerities" catch my ear. I forget there's a cigarette in my hand until it's burned down to the filter and heating my fingers. The men have left and Paula grabs my empty hand, swings it back and forth and asks if I'm having fun yet. I drop the butt and stomp it out. Paula picks it off the ground and sets it in the designated ashcan nearby.

~

Later, as I walk to the car for my water bottle, I hear my name. Damien stops me and asks if I liked the set. I tell him it was great.

"I noticed you ducked out partway through."

"I was there, I just moved to the shade. You must not have seen me."

He nods and looks around, as though scanning for fans. "So, are you still on your *moon time*?"

I laugh and ask if he had the farm breakfast this morning, mention that I helped make it.

"I had some eggs, but it was like noon, so they were cold."

A pickup truck drives by with a group bouncing around in the bed. The driver yells out that they're going to the lake. "Climb aboard!"

I step up, pull myself onto the back of it.

"Bye?" Damien's face is scrunched in disapproval. If I've offended him, I'm not sure. It might be the shrooms, but I no longer care. The truck pulls away and I wave at him through the kicked-up dust.

Hopping on a random truck felt cinematic in the moment. Necessary, even. But now I'm surrounded by people I don't know, on the way to the lake without a bathing suit. My shoulder brushes the arm of the guy next to me, but he's engrossed in a conversation with a person I realize is his identical twin. It must be incredible, I think, to talk to someone who looks and sounds like you but isn't you. No wonder they ignore me. They have each other. I sink down against the side of the truck and look up at the trees. We've pulled off onto the main road, so we'll be at the lake shortly. Maggie and I swam there last year. I realize now it was my favorite part of the weekend: the peace, the nature, the lack of self-consciousness around the comfort of a best friend. I miss her now. I wish she was here.

When we arrive, I ask the driver how long we'll be here. He says maybe half an hour to an hour. "Just a quick dip." I tell him my name and make him promise not to leave without me. He chuckles and says not to worry. He tucks his long hair behind his ears and smirks like he's never worried about a thing.

I remove my pants, leaving on my tank top and underwear. There's no one to egg me on as I wade into the water, so I have to urge myself to jump in. I swing my arms back and forth as I count down. The bottom of the small lake is a mixture of rocks and silt and algae. The unpleasant sensation is a motivator to get my feet out of the muck. I skim the surface as I dive in. When I emerge, I'm yelping from the cold. The twins nearby laugh at my sounds, then toss me their foam football. We pass it around until I'm bored. I hear loons calling from across the lake. The light is golden as the sun teeters into setting. It turns the surface of the water into a mirror. The air cools, and the lake now feels warmer in comparison. I crouch down to dip my body up to my neck, then swim out towards the center, into deeper waters. Treading here, I hear his voice. My chest shudders and my stomach sinks. I look around and spot Tyler on the far end of the beach. He steps into the water. I move my arms faster and treading feels more impossible, like the waters have become a cyclone. I think of Charybdis and try to swim out of it, to get my feet onto the ground again.

I'd been trying so hard not to think about him. The weed and alcohol and mushrooms and capsule of whatever had helped. But now I can't ignore him. His voice bounces off the lake. Still water carries with such clarity.

What is wrong with me why do I feel this way it wasn't that big a deal only a handful of times maybe forty five collective minutes of my life forty five minutes of violation but it's been stretched like a long shadow over me since and somehow this convulsing in my chest is familiar and I can't move my limbs he sees me does he see me is he going to come over here he didn't know it was wrong we were both kids but he was always three years older surely he knew better but everyone goes on living their lives and why should I ruin everything for my entire family by making a big deal of this get over it get over it get fucking over it!

He dives in, under the surface, traveling towards me, it seems. My brain makes contact with my muscles again and I stand up, dash out of the water and towards the parked cars. There's a boat hitched to one near the tree line, and I climb into it, crouch down.

Time is warped when you're having a panic attack. My vision is blurry, my right arm is pins and needles. I hug myself and will my heart not to explode. There's a beach towel on the seat and I wrap myself in it, shivering. My pants are on the shore. Not worth it.

"Alex!"

At the sound of my name I crouch down further.

"All aboard! Train's departing!" I hear the crunching of gravel and then see the mint green and rust of the truck roll by.

I pop up from my hiding place and rush to the truck, climb onto the bed, and don't look back. The driver pokes his head out the window and gives me the thumbs up. My shoes are still here. I slip them on and rub my body with the pilfered towel as we ride away. The lake shrinks into a puddle.

~

At the festival, I find Paula laying on her stomach in the tent, reading a battered paperback. "I needed a break," she says when I crawl in.

"Me too." I change into clean underwear, a new shirt, and my hoodie. My pajama pants are my only remaining bottoms, so I put those on, no longer caring that I look like a child on Christmas morning. I ask where Maggie is, and Paula tells me she's doing whippets with members of The Peach Pit Collective.

"Not your thing?"

"I'd like to keep my brain cells intact," Paula smiles. "Or, some of them, anyway."

I ask her if she's still feeling the mushrooms, and she says they never fully kicked in. She only ate two little ones. I admit I can't tell if what I'm feeling is from smoking or sleep deprivation or the mushrooms. I don't mention the panic.

I ask what she's reading, and she shows me the cover. An anthology of short stories. I get under the blankets and ask her if she'll read aloud for me. She skips to the next story and starts at the beginning. Her voice is hushed and comforting. It is describing a grove of blossoming cherry trees. And then I fall asleep.

~

When I wake up, I'm alone. The lamp is on, but the screen window above reveals darkness outside. I'm conflicted about whether to stay here, in a feeling of relative security, or seek out my friends and enjoy our last night here. Try to enjoy it. Either way, my bladder forces me out of the tent. I consider using the "she wee," then decide to look for a log to squat over, the way my mother taught me to pee in the woods. The glow from the tent nearby anchors me as I walk the perimeter, looking for a fallen tree a respectful distance from other tents. I manage to keep myself dry this time.

I hear footsteps nearing as I return to the tent. It's Paula.

"I got us dinner," she says and hands me a paper container. We duck inside.

"Still no Maggie, huh?"

"No, I don't think we'll be seeing much of her tonight."

"That bassist?"

Paula nods. We eat our bland stir frys, seated on our bedding. The brown rice feels good in my stomach.

She gets out a bottle of white wine and unscrews the lid, passes it to me. "Three Buck Chuck?"

"You're too generous."

"Not for you," she smiles, and that crooked tooth reveals itself again, a glint of it matching the glint in her eyes.

"So what happened with that guy?" she asks when I pass the bottle back to her.

"Eh, wasn't really feeling it."

"Really? Maggie was sure you two were banging in his van last night."

I laugh nervously. "No, nothing went that far." I swallow and it sounds so loud to me I'm sure she can hear it. "I always get scared when it starts to…"

"Hm." The sound is curious rather than judgmental. It's a relief to hear. I've imagined the reaction I'd get from Maggie at this confession and it's never so kind. Which is surely why I haven't admitted this to her before. "Have you ever been with a girl?"

I start to laugh, but Paula's face isn't joking.

"Uh—no. I mean, not really." I set down my dinner, decide I'm finished. I take a longer pull of wine. It burns the back of my throat so pleasantly.

"You might find it less scary, is all."

Inadvertently, I smile and look away. When I look back, she's still staring at me, with such seemingly easy confidence. I find my eyes lingering on her mouth.

"Do you want to?" She smirks and sets down her container, grabs the bottle back from me.

I tell her I find the idea interesting. She takes a slug of wine, and then gets onto all fours and crawls towards me. Her knee gets caught in Maggie's sleeping bag, and she swears at the fabric as she untangles it. We laugh. My limbs are not moving but my heart is hummingbird fast. I feel like a vibrating phone inching across a table. I'm moving towards her. Our lips touch. Soft and slick. I grab her waist, fingers drifting between cloth until I hit skin, and I feel a waterfall of blood rushing inside me. Her own hands and lips move slower than I'm used to. We fall onto our sides. Laugh more amid kisses and I feel her breath pulse into my mouth. We are about the same height and size, so it feels easy, everything aligned and leveled. My mind questions this reality as she unzips my hoodie and lifts her shirt. I take off my own and my mouth finds her nipple. One, then the other. She moans and I pull away, then press my chest against her, my body sticking to the places I've just licked. Unafraid now, my fingers drift up her skirt, working over her underwear, until she pulls it aside for me to feel her slickness. My fingers nestle in around her clit. I push away the thoughts that threaten insecurities of my inexperience and keep going. Her hot muscles spasm. She cries. I hold my hand there and slow until she's finished. She's kissing my neck now. Then she lowers her aim. I notice the carbonated feeling of my skin. As her lips lower down my abdomen, heat floods my core. She tugs on my pants, and I lift my hips, help her get them off. Then her tongue is between my legs. I close my eyes and see colors, hear words: *Ethereal, aquatic, ohmygod.* I gasp and shudder. I'm surprised when I'm coming; this feeling never before shared in someone else's presence, let alone under someone else's control. When I'm done, I sense a light gust. I notice the open screened window overhead and regain consciousness of the world outside this tiny tent, which for a while felt so expansive.

I pull up my pajama pants. "Thank you," the words croak out of me without premeditation.

"Don't mention it." A grin slides over her face. She says she's going to get more water and use the bathroom, that she'll be back in a minute.

I get dressed and wrap myself in the blanket, cold now that I'm alone. When I hear footsteps approaching, I try to look busy. I don't want to seem like I was just sitting here, waiting for her. But when the tent zips open again it's Maggie. She's talking a mile a minute about the band she hung out with and the bassist. I smile and say "Cool," "Cool," "Awesome," "Sounds fun."

"No, but seriously, Alex, seriously–" She's drunk; she clutches my shoulders and pulls me close. I hope she can't see it on my face, what I've just done with her other best friend. "I mean, he's so fucking sexy!" She's babbling about him even as she brushes her teeth, sticks her head out the door to spit. She flattens her rumpled sleeping bag and pulls half the blanket off me, then yanks the end of my shirt to let me know she wants to spoon. Soon, Maggie is snoring. I hear the tent zip open again and I close my eyes too, pretend to doze off. I listen to Paula shuffling around, taking off her glasses, opening a pill bottle, taking a drink of water. Her movements sound routine, like nothing out of the ordinary has just taken place. I try to hear some indication of excitement or regret, as though I could analyze the way she slides into her sleeping bag, adjusts her pillow. She shuts off the lamp, and the backs of my eyelids darken further. She cuddles into the other side of Maggie. I listen for her breathing over Maggie's snores, but it's hard to pinpoint.

~

In the morning, I'm first to wake up again. I'm grateful to not be confronted with opened eyes before I get my bearings. I take a walk to the kitchen. This time they have their fourth and the food is already set out. I move through the line and help myself to a bowl of oats. I spot Damien already at a picnic table, laughing with his bandmates, along with a couple other guys his age. He appears unbothered. I don't know whether to feel hurt or grateful. I take a seat far from his table. There's a family next to me in matching straw sun hats. The toddler stands on the bench and picks fruit from his father's plate. I watch them as I eat spoonfuls of my breakfast, my insides warming. A fly lands on my bowl, but I let it be. There are only so many things I can control, should control. Nearby, a lap steel guitar begins to slide, the sound of it uncertain and lovely.

Acknowledgments

"Boys to Men" was first published by *Maudlin House*.

"Waiting" was first published by *Waxwing*.

"If I Said Everything I Thought" was first published by *Pithead Chapel*.

"In Tandem" was first published under the title "Tandem" by *Hobart After Dark (HAD)*.

"Pervert" was first published by *Jellyfish Review*.

"The Dog" was first published by *Oyez Review*.

"Human Song" was first published by *Smokelong Quarterly* and republished by *Short Édition* in both English and Italian languages.

"When a Woman Walks Alone" was first published by *Assignment Magazine*.

"With Gun" was first published by *Tin House*.

Thank you to those who helped make this story collection a reality. Huge gratitude to Josh Dale, Kat Giordano, and the rest of the Thirty West team. Thank you to my agent Ronald Gerber, who has been such a wonderful supporter of my writing over the past couple years, giving so many hours on feedback, reassurance, and advocacy for my writing.

Huge thanks to all of my writer friends who've provided feedback on these stories during the course of many drafts over the past several years: Rebecca van Laer, Rachel Krantz, Katharine Schellman, Phoebe Rusch, Thomas Warren, Susan Klobuchar, Elizabeth Ellen, Meagan Jennett, and Amy Smith. I hope I'm not forgetting anyone because I've come across so many kind and generous writers who've helped me over the years. Special thanks to Rebecca for her constant wisdom and moral support. And to Rachel for keeping me accountable and encouraged every day, and for reminding me that breaks are okay, too. I'm so lucky to have such incredible, talented friends.

I also owe a huge thank you to all the amazing literary journal editors who've worked with me on the stories in this collection that have been previously published: Rose Skelton, Mallory Smart, Kim Magowan, Aaron Burch, Chris James, Joshua Bohnsack, Christopher Allen, Chaya Bhuvaneswar, and Thomas Ross.

Thank you to Hilary Steinitz, for helping me stay emotionally and mentally healthy through the writing and publishing process. Ditto to Prozac.

Thank you to my in-laws, Chuck and Pattie, for their constant support and encouragement.

Thank you to my parents, for instilling in me a love of the natural world, for teaching me to notice the beauty around me, and for showing me how to appreciate a good walk.

Finally, my biggest thank you goes to my husband, Josh Mound, who is the reason I'm still writing. The way you believe in me and my work has kept me going. You inspired me to see myself as capable, my words as important. You've helped me to work through so many of my personal struggles. More importantly, you've loved me unconditionally through it all.

About the Author

Shannon McLeod is the author of the novella, *Whimsy* (Long Day Press, 2021). Her writing has appeared in *Tin House*, *Prairie Schooner*, *Hobart*, and *SmokeLong Quarterly*, among other publications, and has been nominated for Best Small Fictions, Best of the Net, and featured in *Wigleaf* Top 50. Born in Detroit, she now lives in central Virginia. You can find Shannon on her website at www.shannon-mcleod.com

About the Publisher

Thirty West Publishing House
Handmade chapbooks (and more) since 2015
www.thirtywestph.com / thirtywestph@gmail.com
You should follow us! Consider being a patron?
Review our books on Amazon & Goodreads
@thirtywestph